I0546415

THE
REALM
OF
DARK AND
LIGHT

BOOK THREE:
IN THE HEART OF DARKNESS

THE REALM OF DARK AND LIGHT

BOOK THREE: IN THE HEART OF DARKNESS

PATRICIA PERRY

Riverhaven Books

www.RiverhavenBooks.com

Printed in the United States of America
by Country Press, Lakeville, Massachusetts

Designed and edited by Stephanie Blackman,
Riverhaven Books
Whitman, MA

This book is dedicated to Jerine P. Watson.
Thank you for everything, Big Nurse!

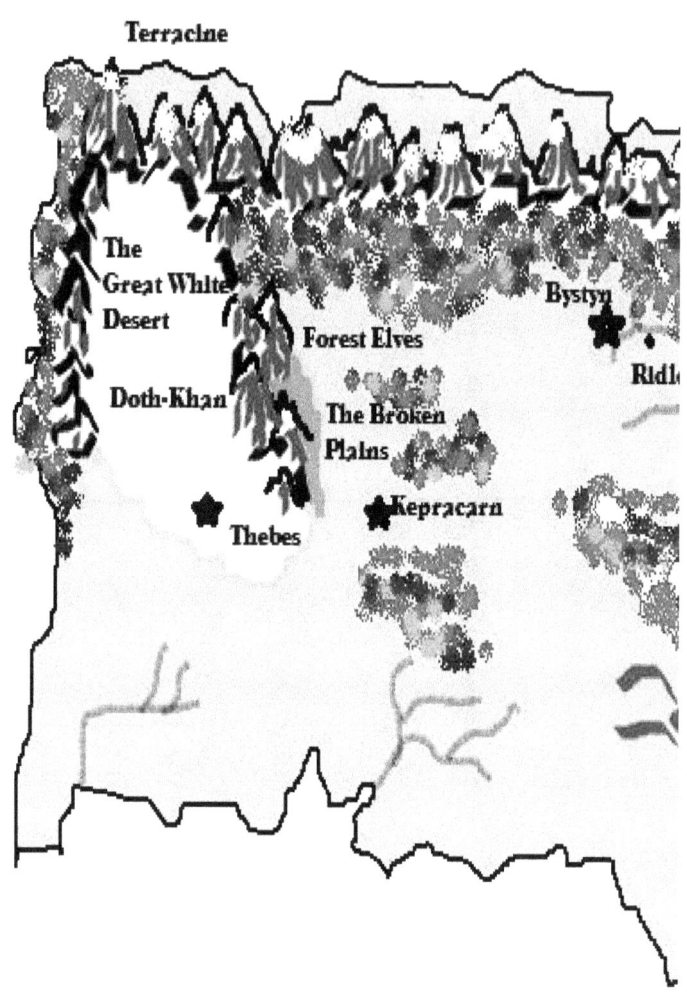

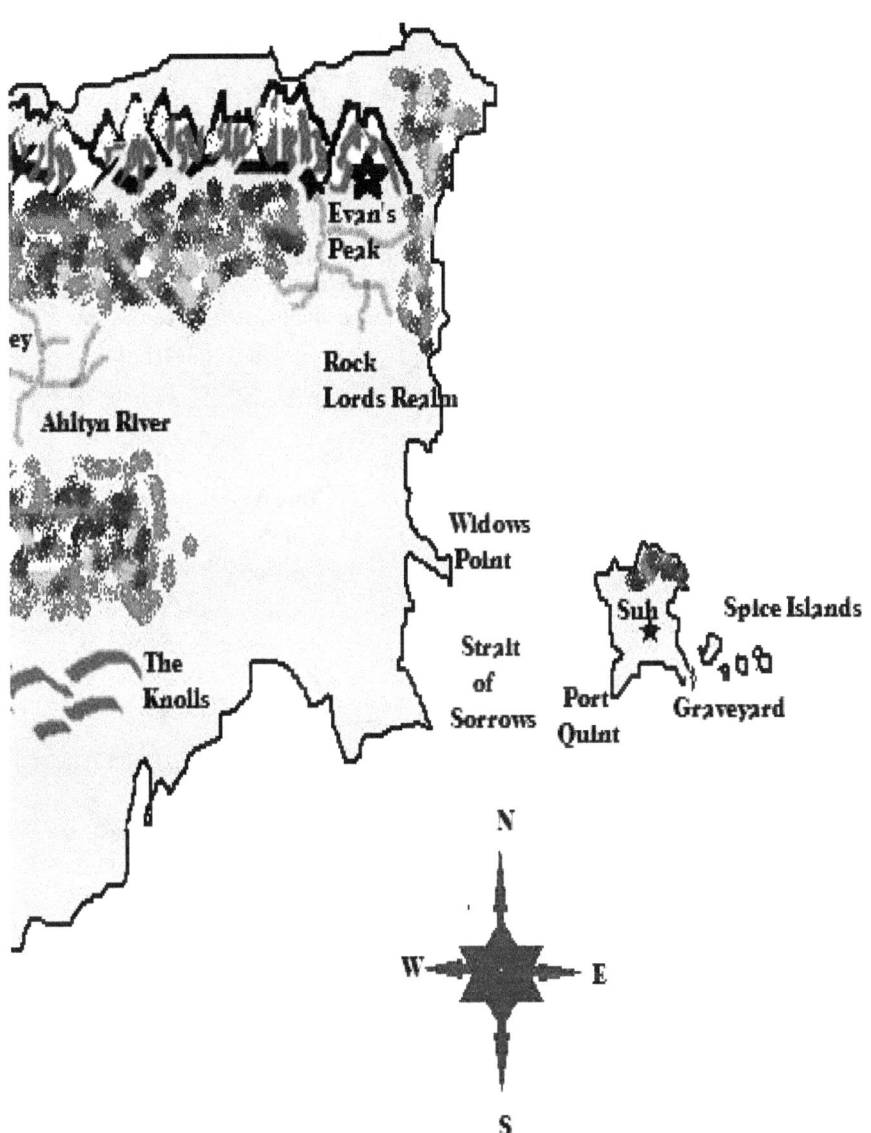

CAST OF CHARACTERS

The Elves
King Alyxandyr I - First Elven King
King Alyxandyr II - Current King
Crown Prince Styph
Prince Nyk – Deceased
Prince Danyl - Bearer of the Green Might
Princess Alyssa
Historian Karolauren (Deceased)
Captain Lance - Danyl's Personal Guard (Deceased)
Captain Drand - Nyk's Personal Guard

Man
King Cooper - Current King of Kepracarn
Mason - Cooper's Brother; Alyxandyr's Advisor
Sophie - Sister of Cooper and Mason
Anci - Sophie and Tabryn's Daughter
Cricket - Orphan; Stole Blue Stone

The Thebans
Oma - Ramira's Friend and Mentor
Imhap - Ramira's Friend and Tutor
Horemb - Theban General; Ramira's Trainer
Ina - Theban High Priestess

The Caldonians
Captain Wil Bloodguard
Captain Jules
Suh - Necromancer
Tong - Suh's Servant
Osgood - Pirate

The Dwarves
King Seven
Queen Clare

The Herkahs
Zada - Leader
Allad - Leader

The Demons
Mahn- Defeated by the
   Allies
Ramira- Bearer of the
   Source of Darkness
Ush-Tak- Vox - deceased
Sul-Tak- Vox current
   leader of the Brethren

The Wraiths
Zaura - Wil's Mother
Zordana
Zimun- Leader
Zulant- a.k.a. Abby
Zistak

PROLOGUE

A little more than a year has passed since the Black Queen defeated the wraith Zulant within Doth-Khan. The battle destroyed the demon lair and forced the Brethren ever northward and beyond the great mountain range. The trek back is arduous and filled with danger, yet the demons' single-minded determination to return to the land and seek revenge on Ramira drives them on.

Reevaluating his plans to obtain the Green Might, Suh finalizes his strategies on Caldon Island. Tong and Jules remain in Bystyn where they keep a watchful eye on Danyl and Wil and report back to the necromancer.

Jules, however, has other ideas. She crafts her own schemes to circumvent Suh and amass the power for herself. Her thoughts are also never far from Danyl, the only man to ever reject her advances.

The collision course between the demons and mortals is about to occur.

PART ONE

ONE

Sunset bathed the desert in warm shades of oranges and reds. Zada eyed the yellowish haze that still hovered over the ruins of Doth-Khan. The demon lair was no more, but the Ankh-Nam remained buried beneath tons of rock and sand.

The Herkah shivered, more from the amulets' presence rather than the chill wind stirring the sands. The demons' existence was inextricably linked to the talisman. The only way to rid the land of the Brethren was to destroy the Ankh-Nam. That, however, meant Ramira's end, too.

Arms encircled her from behind; she placed her hands on Allad's forearms.

"The danger has not passed, Allad."

The eerie vapor undulating in the distance filled his vision. His imprisonment within that toxic morass while possessed by the Vox nearly broke his spirit. The nomad survived by clinging to his love for Zada and his friends.

Allad thought of Horemb. The Theban general's influence on Ramira manifested itself in her extraordinary fighting skills. He was also the first person to be possessed by the high demons. Ramira released his soul by killing him down in the southlands after Mahn flushed her out of Bystyn years before. Horemb managed to retain his sanity for a thousand years with one of the loathsome parasites occupying his body. Allad did not think he could have suffered the Vox for that length of time.

"If Abby sensed the Ankh-Nam's power, then why not the necromancer?"

"Abby was a wraith and could sense the talisman's power," she stated quietly. "Suh is human and isn't tuned into it like she was."

"What about his potions? Couldn't he harness the amulet's magic with them?"

3

"His potions would be incapable of controlling the talisman's evil power."

"It would destroy him."

"Yes," she turned and laid her head against his shoulder.

"We must dig it up and obliterate it, Zada."

"There is only one who can do that, Allad."

"Well," he led her back to their tent, "at least its location is known only to a handful of people."

"We still have to be vigilant, Allad."

"That's something to share with our friends when we meet for the autumn festival."

"Indeed."

Streaks of reds, oranges, and lavenders stained the horizon as the quarter moon rose in the darkening sky. The desert reflected the fiery hues and then transformed into a sea of sparkling white. The desert became silent and cold prompting the nomads to seek the warmth of their tent. Allad looked back at the faint yellowish smudge for a moment and shivered before securing the tent flap.

Shaking in the pre-dawn hours woke the nomads. They darted out of their tents and stared at the fog rising over the ruins of Doth-Khan. Pinpoints of amber light flashing within the swirling vapor were visible even from this distance. The gyrating column expanded with every pulse, forcing its leading edge toward the nomads. Horses panicked and bolted; the Herkahs shouted out in confusion.

Zada couldn't breathe; her face lost all color. She clung to Allad who struggled to remain on his feet as the tremors continued to swell outward from Doth-Khan. Then, as quickly as the quakes began, they subsided.

Allad looked questioningly at Zada.

Zada shook her head in response, an uneasy feeling gripping her heart.

~

The ground within the ruins of Doth-Khan angled eastward. Rocks loosened by the vibrations fell into the pocket holding Ush-Tak's skeletal remains. Dislodged by the boulders rolling over the corpse, the Ankh-Nam slid toward the crevasse less than a foot away from the dead Vox. The shuddering bounced it from one narrow ledge to the next until it teetered on the final shelf overlooking an underground waterway. It dangled for a few seconds then plunged into the black river below. The amulet landed on a branch that floated in an easterly direction.

∼

Zada's inner sight opened. The blackness to the north wavered for a moment before she could see the complete ruins of the demon lair. Its black heart, however, was gone. A faint trace marked its journey eastward. Hazy impressions identified the demons. They survived but were too far away for her to locate with any certainty. It was as if something blocked them from her inner sight. The nomad retreated from the in-between world.

"Zada?"

"Doth-Khan is completely sealed, Allad," she said while accepting his support.

"The amulet?"

"It is gone."

"Destroyed?"

"No…on its way east."

"How is that possible, Zada?"

"I don't know."

"What of the demons?"

"They exist on the very edges of my inner sight, Allad."

"Why don't we head for Bystyn sooner than we planned?"

Allad felt her nod her head against his shoulder.

∼

Sul-Tak eyed the snowy wasteland on the other side of the mountain range. The Vox had assumed the leadership role after Ush-Tak's death in Doth-Khan. Sul-Tak despised Mee-La for her duplicity and vowed to seek revenge on her.

The Black Queen's treachery resonated amongst the Brethren as they, too, sought her death. The demons' first priority, however, was to return to the land.

The Brethren scoured the numerous caverns for a way back. They discovered promising routes that always ended in a barrier. The Kreetch's smaller forms and clawed hands were better suited to maneuver over and around the mountains' irregularities.

Sul-Tak watched an animated Kreetch jump up and down while it pointed back at the fissure behind them.

"There is a way through," wheezed Sul-Tak.

The trek would be grueling; remaining stagnant disastrous. He assessed the Brethren's condition: the demons needed to eat. His attention was drawn to a herd of deer near the forest line. Curious of the newcomers, the animals remained motionless but alert when a group of demons approached them.

The Brethren took their time surrounding the herd then surged forward as one. The demons swarmed the deer that hesitated; the rest of the demons joined in for the kill. The Brethren dragged the carcasses closer to the foot of the mountain, leaving garish streaks on top of the snow.

"When do you want to leave, Sul-Tak?"

The Vox ignored the bright red stains and trampled snow. "When everyone is sated."

Sul-Tak accepted a chunk of meat from one of the Kreetch. He studied the gap in the mountain and then scrutinized the mount's face. The nearly vertical gray stone stretched upward for more than a mile; the sheer contours offered no footing. Licking his fingers, the Vox scanned the range from west to east. The impenetrable wall of gray continued well beyond his sight. His attention returned to the cleft. It was their only way back to the land. Sul-Tak waved over one of the

Vox.

"How many did Brethren did we lose during our march?"

"More than two dozen," it rasped.

"We'll replace them once we return to the other side."

The high demon nodded and resumed its tasks.

Sul-Tak's attention returned to the massive range. Would they find a way back? If so, how far to the east or west were they? Sul-Tak thought of the Ankh-Nam. The venerated amulet remained buried within Doth-Khan.

The Brethren will recover you, he silently vowed.

A disheveled Suh stared with red-rimmed eyes at the dozens of open books strewn across every available surface. Somewhere within those thousands of pages was a spell that could grant him more power. In the meantime, he needed more wraith blood. Returning to the Wold in the far northwest region was not an option, but what if a wraith wandered somewhere on Caldon Island? Or the mainland? Would he be able to find Abby? He plucked the last vial of wraith blood from his pocket and held it up to his face: it was half full.

Suh poured himself a glass of wine and ventured outside. He had returned to the island a month ago, searching for an incantation to bolster his power. His fruitless results grated on his nerves. The sooner he could secure the Elven magic, the faster he could implement his plans. The necromancer wondered what Jules and Tong gleaned from their reconnaissance in Bystyn. The last dispatch from them revealed nothing unusual occurring in the city.

The necromancer surveyed his property. His desire to abandon it was in the forefront of his mind. The mainland was vast and the possibilities endless. He could still control Caldon Island and Widows Point if he assigned the right individuals to oversee them. All he had to do was find that elusive spell and commence with his schemes.

Suh drained his glass and returned to his chamber. He leaned back against the counter with crossed arms and skimmed the books. "Such a powerful spell would be hidden or disguised."

He walked over to the books, willing the yellowed pages to reveal their secrets. "Obscure, complicated or obvious…where would it be? Where would *I* place it?"

A fragrant breeze blowing in through the open windows stirred the pages. The necromancer glared at the books that refused to yield their secrets to him. Frustrated, Suh pushed all the books off the counter. Muttering under his breath, he picked them up. A thin volume caught his interest. He read the title: *Arturus Dimand.* Suh leafed through pages filled with exquisitely drawn plants, insects, and split rocks bursting with colored crystals inside. A list of ingredients and words in an unknown language were written on the last page. Thirty-four objects: only seven were necessary for this particular spell. Was this it? If so, how was he supposed to know which elements, and in what quantity, would work? Suh knew better than to randomly combine the ingredients.

"Suh?"

The necromancer motioned for the messenger to enter. The man placed numerous packages on the counter and then handed the necromancer a sealed letter. Suh placed the envelope on the counter and then emptied the parcels on the bench. He sorted through Abby's belongings while wondering what had happened to her after she escaped from Caldon Island with the others. Neither Tong nor Jules mentioned her in any of their letters, so she was not in the Elven city. Was she wandering around the mainland somewhere? The wraith certainly hadn't returned to the island.

Suh inventoried the glass containers filled with powders, herbs, and colored liquids. He separated the ingredients he recognized from those he did not. Another satchel held a leather-bound book written in a neat but foreign script. The third bag contained her hair brush and bottles of lotion. He uncorked the containers and sniffed their contents. All but one smelled of flowers. It had a lemony aroma. Suh pursed his lips in thought, for that scent stirred a distant memory. Try as he might, the necromancer could not recall it. Frustrated, he picked up the letter.

"This island is full of that scent," he muttered to himself while breaking the wax seal. It was from Tong.

Abby accompanied the Herkahs west and has not been seen since. There was some sort of turmoil there not long afterward, but no one speaks of it. Bloodguard is spending a great deal of time with the Elven prince.

"Bloodguard? I thought I killed that bastard a year ago!" growled Suh, then continued to read.

We know where Bloodguard lives and that he heads for the castle every morning. Bloodguard is a frequent guest at the elf's home. The elf has a woman and two children. Will you be returning before autumn? Do you have any further instructions for us?

Tong

"Hmm…perhaps the elf would be more cooperative if his woman or children are in my hands."

Suh looked at the open books then over to Abby's things. He picked up the *Arturus Dimand* and absently thumbed through the pages. He closed the book then studied the spine. The letters were stamped in gold. The necromancer turned the book over and studied the closed pages. Also gold. Suh held it up to the light and squinted at the faint smudges along the edges of the paper. He flipped the front and back covers away from the pages then bent the sheets without separating them. Seven images appeared.

"Very clever!" he proclaimed.

On a whim, he gently twisted the top and bottom of the pages. A cold smile played on his face as he beheld the exact measure of each item. Suh wrote everything down then checked his supplies for the ingredients. He was missing one component.

"Where am I going to find Demon's Breath?"

Suh knew one person who could tell him.

"Guard!"

"Suh?"

"We're setting out for Widows Point before nightfall. Send word to Graveyard that I want the *Gray Wolf* ready to sail the moment we arrive."

"Yes, Suh."

The necromancer packed some personal items, the *Arturus Dimand*, and a generous supply of potions. His men hauled the satchels to the waiting horses and headed for Graveyard.

The sun beat down upon the travelers from a cloudless sky. Sweating freely, their tunics stuck to their upper bodies. The humidity increased the closer they rode to the shoreline. This time of year was the most oppressive and even riding beneath the trees did nothing to ward off the sweltering heat. The briny ocean breeze made little impact on their discomfort.

They continued on the worn trail down to Graveyard. Most of the town had been rebuilt following Suh's fiery assault nearly two years ago, although the charred remains of some buildings remained. Suh urged his mount toward Bloodguard's old office and dismounted. He ignored the pirates flanking the doorway and entered the room. Osgood removed his feet from the corner of the desk and stood up.

"Da *Gray Wolf* is ready ta sail, Suh."

The necromancer took the sheet of paper from Osgood and scanned the cargo list. Spices, marinated shellfish, and exotic fruits promised a healthy sum at the end of the trip. He glanced at the books on the window sill behind the pirate then retrieved them. Opening one of them revealed a neat script. Bloodguard's handwriting. Suh added the books to his satchel and then headed down to the pier. The *Gray Wolf* bobbed languidly against the dock. Sailors scrambled in the rigging while others loaded up the last of the crates and barrels from the wharf. Suh approached the gangplank and shoved one of the seamen out of his way as he boarded the ship. He climbed up to the captain's cabin and deposited his things on the bunk.

The necromancer walked out on the deck and watched the deckhands untie the lines while two men dragged the gangway onto the dock. The *Gray Wolf* lurched forward when several sails were unfurled. He heard the captain barking orders to release more canvas. The ship navigated past the jetties then glided out onto the open sea. The sails snapped then filled with wind.

Suh tapped his index finger on the rail while watching Graveyard disappear behind him. His miscalculation regarding Bloodguard irritated him. He had twice failed to kill the man and the pirate had somehow managed to ingratiate himself with his quarry. That information, along with the possibility of Bloodguard or Abby recognizing him, forced him to reassess his plans. At least, according to Tong's last dispatch, Bloodguard had not identified his spies.

Suh returned to the cabin and leafed through Bloodguard's books. Tides, currents, water depths, and towns were meticulously drawn and noted throughout the pages. Suh offered the pirate a praiseworthy nod when he scanned the inventory sections. Every piece of merchandise was listed with its value down to the last coin. The necromancer tossed the books onto the bunk and picked up the *Arturus Dimand*. Leafing through the pages, Suh was impressed with the incredible details in the drawings. Someone with a steady hand and great eye illustrated every feature to perfection. The necromancer yawned. Stowing the books in his satchel, Suh blew out the lantern and fell asleep.

~

The *Gray Wolf* finally docked near sunset two days later, an impatient Suh debarking with one of his bags before the gangplank was secured. The necromancer followed the winding back streets to a grimy building in a murky quarter. He entered the shop and knocked on the stained wooden counter. Heavy incense and musty odors assailed his nostrils; a pair of yellow eyes staring unblinkingly at him from a shadowy corner caught his attention. An ancient woman with wild gray hair walked through the dusty curtains. She rested her gnarled hands on the counter; her milky eyes looked right through him.

"I need a certain ingredient."

"What ya need?"

"Demon's Breath. Do you have any?"

Unease rippled through the old woman, for that component was used for only one spell. "Dat's forbidden, Suh."

He started when the ancient collection of rags and dust that called him by name. "I don't care. I need it."

"Ya won't git it 'ere."

The necromancer searched the rows of shelves behind her. None of the containers were marked. One of those glass vials had to be filled with Demon's Breath. He looked back at the old woman.

"If ya want dat, ya 'ave to get it yerself, Suh."

"Which bottle holds Demon's Breath, Witch?"

"Dere ain't no bottle strong enough ta hold dat evil."

"Where can I get it, then?"

"Why ya want ta make da Unspeakable, Suh?"

"Because I *can*, old woman. Now, where can I get it?"

"West."

"That narrows it down." His voice dripped with sarcasm.

"Da demon will find ya 'fore you find it."

Suh glared at the witch then turned to go. An image of Bloodguard in the glade formed in his mind. The necromancer approached the counter once more.

"Do you have any potions that have a lemony smell?"

"Jus' one."

"And that would be?"

"An aphrodisiac," she replied.

That was the last type of potion he would have guessed. "Who purchased it?"

"Cap'n Bloodguard."

The necromancer pursed his lips when she confirmed his suspicions. "When?"

"About a year ago."

"For whom did he buy it?"

"Fer a special lady."

"Yes, but who was she?"

"He didn't say."

The old woman watched him leave, his demand for Demon's Breath echoing in her mind. The necromancer had discovered the spell for a power that had long been hidden for a good reason. How he came across the book was a mystery; what she had to do was not. She tapped the countertop with a crooked finger. Wisps of gray hair floated around her head as the cool night air seeped in through a broken window pane. Candles of varying sizes sat in their own drippings; the breeze disturbed their flames. Unblinking yellow eyes continued to glow from within the shadows. The old woman abruptly selected six vials from the shelves and placed them on the counter.

"You seek something that is well beyond your capability to control, necromancer," she muttered. "I will witness the destruction of both you and the one who killed my sister."

She mumbled a series of slurred words. A grayish vapor enveloped her and then vanished. A plain woman with black hair and eyes appeared; her movements were bird-like. She carefully wrapped the bottles with cloth before placing them inside a bag.

"Let's go see what Suh is up to, Ceela."

The yellow eyes finally blinked.

Having left the shop, Suh walked to the inn. His mind was filled with two things: Demon's Breath and Bloodguard. He decided to focus on Bloodguard first. An aphrodisiac? What would Bloodguard want with a love potion? The man was known to bed any woman he wanted. Who did he meet that was unwilling or unable to sleep with him? The necromancer marched up to his suite without acknowledging the guards in the hallway. He poured himself a glass of wine and sat out on the balcony. A full moon lit up the seafront; a cool breeze chased away the heat and humidity. His thoughts returned to Bloodguard.

"Why would a man of your abilities need to drug a woman? Who is she? Why would she spurn your advances? No woman in Graveyard would reject you. A stranger? From the mainland? Someone you met when you escaped Caldon Island?"

The necromancer drained his glass and refilled it, the mystery surrounding Bloodguard's unknown love interest resonating in his mind. He wanted to solve this before he could concentrate on the Demon's Breath.

"I found you in the woods a short ride away from the Elven city," he continued, taking another sip of wine. "Was it a woman from that city? Did you plan on meeting her or was it happenstance?"

Shouting in the streets broke into his thoughts. Unflattering words were exchanged and then a woman screamed for the constabulary. A dog growled nearby; a man slurred the words to a song. Suh thought back to the strangers. There was a dwarf and the elf whose power he coveted. Were they the ones at Abby's house who killed his men? No…Tong said that there was a man and a woman at her home. He saw none of the strangers when he attacked Graveyard, but there was an incident involving a strange woman before he arrived. She defeated Doomah and thereby gained her freedom. No, that wasn't quite correct. She and the others escaped when he invaded Graveyard. Abby fled to Graveyard with the two outsiders, Tong in pursuit. They all boarded the *Gray Wolf* and sailed away from Caldon Island.

Bloodguard is spending a great deal of time with the Elven prince.

Suh sat on the edge of the bench. Jules commanded the *Gray Wolf* and would be able to identify the woman and maybe even her relationships with the other outsiders. The necromancer knew he would have to be careful when questioning her.

"What prompted you to venture west, Captain Bloodguard? Perhaps a better question would be *who*?"

TWO

Ramira thought about Wil Bloodguard's heritage. His mother, Zaura, was the third wraith who had accompanied Zistak and Zulant to Suh's enclosure. Zaura kept this hidden from her son to protect him from men like Suh, and even from himself. She instilled principles in him and insisted that he become a learned man. These beliefs resurfaced once he disconnected himself from Graveyard's influence and embraced his life in Bystyn. No one left alive could link him to his heritage, but did his wraith side - like her demon legacy - connect him to his origin? What sort of creatures were these wraiths?

Zaura and Zistak displayed goodness while Zulant chose to be evil. Wil's mother took great care to insulate him from his heritage. Zistak, according to Zulant, never condemned her evil sister for her betrayal.

Ramira was forced to abandon her thoughts to tend to her child, Wyl. She picked him up and nursed him. Kayla played with her toes in her crib; Blue curled up on the bed beside Ramira.

"Half-demon, one-quarter man, and one-quarter wraith," she whispered to her son, "with a full-blooded elf as your adoptive father."

Ramira looked into his eyes and lost herself in the waves of blue topped with white foam. She could almost smell the ocean and feel the wind tugging on her hair and clothes. She caressed his back with her fingertips and offered him a little smile.

"Fate cannot get enough of complicating our lives, can she?"

"Ramira?" Sophie called out to her. "Are you ready to go?"

"I'll be down in a few minutes!"

Ramira placed her now sleeping son in the linen shawl that she draped around her shoulder and then scooped up her daughter. Blue padded down the stairs and went over to Sophie, who scratched the cat behind her ears.

"Here." Sophie held out her hands and said, "I'll take Kayla."

Sophie and Ramira turned down one of the side streets in the western half of Bystyn, their destination a shop selling a variety of herbs, jams, and other condiments. Sophie carried Kayla while Wyl continued to nap in the wrap. The sun warmed the lane that stretched from the western walls to the square. An outdoor teashop at the edge of the square beckoned to the women.

"Shall that be our last stop, Ramira?"

"As long as these two behave."

Sophie chuckled and entered the store; Ramira sat on a bench in front of the building. Shops, taverns, and rooms for rent were sprinkled on both sides of the street to the end of the block; family-owned homes began at the next quarter. An inn, where a woman cranked open the striped awnings and then rearranged the tables, was located directly across the street. The brown-haired elf smiled and waved to Ramira, who returned the greeting.

Ramira watched the passersby, the canopy hanging over the storefront providing shade from the sun. She glanced down at her son who slept peacefully within the linen shawl. He was Wil's pride and joy, yet he never gave any hint that the baby was his son. Ramira could not fathom how difficult that must be for him. She and Danyl encouraged Wil to spend a lot of time at their home. The mutual respect felt by all three flourished into a friendship that benefitted everyone, especially Kayla and Wyl. The brigand spent equal time with both children, loving them as if they were his own. Ramira understood his innate feelings. She, like Wil, had been bereft of a family for a very long time.

Ramira had heard the whispered gossip as to how this stranger had endeared himself to her family. Wil's numerous visits and his informal manner produced more opinions than she could count. She also heard the rumors from the young women who found his looks and charm irresistible. Ramira smiled, for one fortunate woman would eventually steal Wil's attention. She closed her eyes and sighed, allowing the tranquility of the moment to enfold her. A slight smile turned up the corners of her mouth as the scent of sun-warmed skin, leather, and faint traces of soap drifted toward her.

"Good morning, Pirate," she quietly greeted him.

"How did you know it was me?"

Ramira opened her eyes and waved him to the seat beside her.

Wil winked at her in response. He peeked at his son then lightly ran his index finger across the baby's cheek, oblivious of the woman watching him from across the street. His gaze traveled to the knives prominently strapped to Ramira's thighs, a deadly warning to anyone foolish enough to attempt harming her children. Her retribution would make even the Black Queen blanch.

"Are you alone?"

"No," she replied shifting the baby to a more comfortable position. "Sophie and Kayla are inside."

Two women walked by and nodded at Ramira before focusing their attention on the handsome man beside her.

"Good morning, Wil!" they said in unison.

"Good day to you two lovely ladies!"

The brown-haired elf shook her head while covering the tables with white linens. She disappeared into the tavern then reemerged with a tray of napkins, glasses, and silverware.

"Tell me, Pirate, how many maidens will you defile before you find the one who suits you?"

Wil leaned toward Ramira and conspiratorially whispered, "I've already sullied that woman, but she won't have me anymore."

"How unfortunate."

"She broke my heart."

"Ah… poor Pirate."

Wil glanced across the way and noticed the smirking elf wrapping napkins around sets of silverware. Ramira followed his gaze and bit her lower lip to keep from laughing.

"Does she find me amusing?"

"I think so."

The woman turned the glasses upside down near the flatware all the while ignoring Wil's sudden interest in her.

He rested his elbows on his knees and studied the elf that refused to acknowledge him.

Ramira found it hard to keep a straight face.

"Maybe I'll eat a meal there tomorrow," he mumbled out loud.

"Why? Do you think she'll stop laughing by then?"

"Is the 'sullied' woman jealous?" he whispered into her ear.

"Please."

"Has the 'sullied' woman forgotten my *talents*?"

"They were adequate," she replied in bored tones.

"Just 'adequate'?"

Ramira shrugged indifferently.

"I distinctly remember…."

Kayla reached out for Wil when Sophie carried her and her goods over to them.

"Come here, Buttercup!"

Wil collected Kayla in his arms and delighted in the kisses the little girl planted on his cheek. She hugged his neck; Wil laughed and tickled her.

"I'm ready for some tea," said Sophie.

The baby stirred within the shawl, so Ramira arranged herself to discreetly nurse him as they headed toward the tables.

Another woman batted her eyes at Wil as she walked by. The brigands' smile made her turn around.

"Will you join us?" asked Sophie.

"I'd love to, but I'm suffocating beneath the adoration of all these women!"

"Don't encourage him," Ramira said, sitting down while lifting two fingers to the server.

"I'll be on my way now. It's been a pleasure, ladies," he said, winking at them before disappearing down one of the narrow lanes connected to the main avenue.

Ramira checked on her children and then watched the elves go about their business. A boy wearing baggy clothing caught her attention. There was something familiar about him but his shaggy bangs concealed most of his face as he crossed the plaza and entered a shop on the corner. Sipping her tea and chatting with Sophie made her forget the nagging feeling.

~

Jules watched the women from a shop diagonally across the street. She pretended to browse, but her focus was on Wil strolling down one of the alleyways. She made a mental note then concentrated on Ramira, the children, and the other woman sitting beneath the awning outside the tea shop. The little girl was about a year old; she was clueless about the baby wrapped in the shawl.

Jules stared at the knives secured to Ramira's thighs. Visions of Ramira burying them in Allad's chest played out in front of her. Rather than dying, the man was somehow revived. Did they have any special power? Could she tap into that magic? Jules thought about revealing the knives' importance to Suh then discarded that notion. She would collect and keep any leverage for her own use.

The women left and Jules was about to return to her room when Wil reappeared from one of the side streets. Jules left the shop and casually sauntered over to the lane. She pretended to look in the storefronts while trying to determine what drew Wil down this street. The building to her right was the main entrance to the tavern facing the shop Ramira and Wil had occupied earlier. The two-story house to the left accommodated a condiment vendor and a baker. Private residences began at the end of the block.

Through the reflection in the window, Jules saw Wil wave to an elf sweeping the stoops and surrounding walkway. She responded with a brief nod and continued her task. The woman offered him a tight smile and then entered the tavern when he persisted in conversing with her. Wil hesitated then headed toward the square. Jules stared coldly at his retreating back.

~

19

Jules returned to the cramped room near sunset. Tong sat on his bed reading the latest dispatch from Suh. Jules stepped out onto the balcony and sat on a squat bench. Vegetation blocked her view of the buildings across from her.

Wil trying to start a conversation with the elf woman repeated itself in her mind. And the woman spurning Wil's advances did nothing to lessen Jules' irritation. Wil pursued whatever he desired until it became his. Jules played that game with him and almost succeeded in taking everything that belonged to Wil. Only a quick-thinking pirate and the healer Abby foiled her well thought out plans.

"Suh's letter is to the point," Tong called out to her.

Tong's voice pulled her out of her musing. "What does it say?"

"He'll be here within the month."

"It's about time."

Yes, thought Tong, *it is.*

Tong pictured the emerald vegetation and sapphire blue waters of the Spice Islands. The sumptuous feast marking the beginning of a new year would begin soon. He pictured the young women dancing, their deeply tanned bodies clad only in a brightly colored loin cloth. Flower garlands would be draped around their necks; their shiny black hair would reach the small of their backs. The natives lived a simple life, yet one that brimmed with exuberance. Tong spent decades in Suh's service - it was time to enjoy himself. This was his last duty to the necromancer, and he couldn't wait until it was completed.

Tong studied Jules' dour expression. She wanted this over and done with, too, but for different reasons. Jules' lust for power matched only her carnal desires. The captain was a shrewd woman; it wouldn't surprise him if she twisted Suh's plans to further her own. Tong shrugged inwardly. He didn't care what any of them intended after all of this was over. Tong lay on his bed; Jules joined him moments later.

"You're better than nothing," she muttered.

Once a whore, always a whore, he mused.

~

Wil approached the tavern the next day and sat in a chair at the edge of the patio, avoiding the customers occupying the tables near the doorway. He leaned back into the seat and watched the elf walk up to him. The woman placed her hands on her hips and waited for him to order.

"My name is Hanna…what can I get for you?"

"What are the specials today?"

"Roasted chicken and steamed vegetables, smoked fish with a mustard sauce or stew."

Hanna's brown hair hung in a braid down her back; long lashes framed her light brown eyes. A mischievous smile played on her lips.

"What do you recommend, Hanna?"

"The smoked fish with a glass of mountain white."

"I'll have that."

Hanna disappeared into the tavern. She returned a few minutes later with the wine and a pitcher of water. Flipping the glass right side up, she filled it halfway. Wil's casual scrutiny earned him a raised eyebrow.

"My name is Wil."

"I know," she replied in a disinterested tone.

"Is there anyone in this city who *doesn't* know my name?"

"No," she answered and left to tend to her other patrons.

Wil sipped his wine beneath the striped awning. A young woman carrying a basket walked by and greeted him just as Hanna carried over his meal. Wil offered her a polite nod of his head and then turned his focus back to Hanna. She placed his food on the table.

"Would you need anything else?"

"Yes," Wil leaned forward, "will you have dinner with me?"

"I don't socialize with my customers."

"Then I'll never eat here again!"

"You won't after you eat that fish," she replied wiping her hands on her apron.

"Then why did you recommend it?"

"So you would never eat here again," she stated and walked away.

Confusion rippled across his features; his mouth opened but no words came out. Not knowing what else to do, he tentatively took a small bite of the fish: it melted in his mouth. He consumed the meal. Wil pushed the empty plate back and drained his glass when Hanna returned.

"Dessert?"

"Another dish to keep me away?"

"That depends on what you order."

Wil decided to play along. "What do you recommend?"

"Humble pie."

"Ouch."

"It's a lot more palatable with our homemade whipped cream."

"You don't think much of me, do you, Hanna?"

"I don't know you."

"That's what dinners are for."

"Your bill."

Wil hesitated for a second then placed the coins and her tip on the table. "Thank you for your hospitality and, by the way, the fish was delicious."

Hanna collected his dishes while watching him walk toward the main square. One of the diners called out for another ale, breaking the hold Wil's retreating figure had on her.

~

Suh and his men set out from Widows Point at dawn, their destination about two weeks away to the west. He estimated their arrival time around early autumn. The necromancer's mind was consumed with two things: Bloodguard and Demon's Breath. He decided to concentrate on the ingredient this time.

Was this element found somewhere in this land? If so, how would he recognize it? Suh had no idea if it resided in the ground, the water, or in the mountains to the north. The necromancer scrutinized every single page looking for even the remotest of clues but found nothing. Manipulating the pages did not help either. He shook his head.

What if Suh needed to find an actual demon? The old woman told him that the demon would locate him before he it. He revisited the same questions and came up with the same frustrating lack of answers.

The group reined in after sundown and made camp. The brigands tended to the horses and the evening meal. This scene replayed itself for more than a week and a half. The closer they traveled to the northern mountains, the chillier the nights became. The brigands clustered around the fire with their blankets draped across their shoulders while they ate. They eyed the necromancer as he walked away from the camp. One of the pirates mumbled under his breath while propping the blanket up around his neck. Another one shot a sour glance at Suh's retreating back.

Suh studied the star-encrusted heavens. The North Star shone brightly against the inky darkness. The necromancer opened his senses to his surroundings. Night bird tweets and chirping crickets ceased when an animal screeched in the distance. That sound ended as suddenly as it started. He shivered; his breath condensed in front of him.

Demon's Breath…forbidden…the demon will find you first…no bottle can contain that evil…the Unspeakable…

"Why will it find me first?"

He exhaled again. The witch's words echoed in his mind repeatedly. The innkeeper in Ridley told him about the demons when he first traveled to Bystyn. Where did they go? How was he going to find them? Unbidden images of hideous things formed in his mind. Vile creatures assailed humans then returned to their musty lairs, leaving utter destruction in their wake. The demon would tear him apart before he managed to secure a single breath.

Da demon will find ya 'fore you find it.

Suh took a deep breath and headed back to the camp fires. He

23

never noticed a pair of yellow eyes watching him from an overhead branch.

~

Sul-Tak and the demons followed the Kreetch through the mountain. Caverns large enough to house a city shrank until the demons squeezed through narrow fissures. Glowing greenish-white veins illuminated the rock walls; stalagmites and stalactites formed gleaming columns of the same hue. Melting snow gushed through channels far below as the Brethren pushed on. They followed the waterway as it flowed toward the plains and freedom. The laborious trek south caused even the demons to rest. Exhaustion and hunger slowed their pace but not their purpose.

The Brethren's journey was in its seventh day when the mountain began to shake. Several columns collapsed beneath the mountains' shifting weight; tons of rocks clogged their escape. Sul-Tak used his tunic to cover his nose and mouth as the dust settled around them. Wiping the grit from his eyes, the Vox surveyed the scene. The promising way out was completely blocked. Numerous demons lay crushed beneath the debris. Disappointment and disaster mirrored their every step. The Vox surveyed the Brethren who looked to him for leadership. They waited in silence for him to direct them.

~

A faint glow penetrated Ramira's sleep. It hovered on the edge of her perception and immobilized her. She felt helpless. The yellowish vapor surrounded her and began to pour down her throat. Something black swirled within it, something she recognized. Powerless to ward it off, she sensed it closing the distance. A cold wind dispersed the suffocating vapor.

Ramira stood upon a pinnacle of rock and looked down. The soupy fog hid everything below her. She didn't know if the ground was inches below the mist or if she stood on top of a mountain. She shifted her gaze to the sky. A hazy circle of light penetrated through the eerie clouds. Ramira couldn't tell if it was the sun or the moon. Or something else.

The scar on her chest began to itch then burn as the Ankh-Nam sought its rightful place. Memories of the potent magic coursing through her body flared in Ramira's mind. The wind stirred her peculiar attire as she slowly raised her arms up to receive the amulet. Ramira felt its arctic touch when it hung itself around her neck. Panic lodged in her throat as the revolting amulet lay against her skin and resumed its place over her heart. The soft bed transformed into hard rock; the familiar scents were replaced with Sulphur and mustiness. She dared not open her eyes….

Moaning woke Danyl. He glanced over at Ramira and frowned. Sweat beaded up on her face and body even though she lay perfectly still.

"Ramira! Can you hear me?"

Perspiration soaked into her pillow; tears rolled down the sides of her ashen face.

"*Ramira!*"

Ramira heard his voice and instinctively reached for him. A pair of hands latched onto hers and anchored her to reality. She grabbed onto Danyl, who cradled her until she regained control of herself.

"What happened?"

"I…don't know," she panted. "I was someplace dark and the amulet tried to infuse itself in me again."

He forced her to look into his eyes. "You're safe, Ramira." *For now*, he thought while holding her.

~

For the fifth day in a row, Jules hid in the narrow alleyway across from the tavern where Wil sat at his usual table. The elf woman wore a good-natured expression regardless of who she was serving, even toward Wil. His perseverance in pursuing the elf woman, however, infuriated Jules. Especially when he offered her a fresh red rose every day. The woman never picked up any of the flowers. Jules glared at her former lover. Wil had lavished her with gorgeous jewelry and rare silks, but those luxuries were payment for her services both in and out of the bedroom. The simple red rose was given for a completely different reason.

The elf woman disappeared inside the tavern, reemerging moments later with an armful of plates. She deposited them on a table and, after a brief conversation with the four patrons seated there, reentered the tavern.

Wil nonchalantly watched her interact with her customers. The woman returned to his table, ignoring the slight smile he offered her. She placed his meal down and left before he could engage her in small talk.

"She doesn't want you, *my love*," Jules muttered under her breath.

The woman returned after he had eaten and removed his dinnerware.

He took a deep breath and swallowed his disappointment.

Jules sneered at Wil, whose frustration bubbled below the surface. Wil stood up and said something to the elf woman when she returned with his bill. She hesitated for a moment then shook her head. He spoke a few more words; she placed her hands on her hips. The woman stared off into the distance while he continued to speak to her. Finally, after a long silence, she nodded her head. Picking up the coins and the rose, the elf woman entered the tavern.

Wil, Jules noted, wore a delighted and relieved expression on his face.

The coldness radiating from Jules' eyes was fed by the glacial resentment within her soul. "She'll never have you, *my love*."

Jules glared at the woman for several long minutes before returning to her room. Drinking an entire glass of wine in one gulp, she began to formulate a plan in her mind. She didn't turn around when Tong entered the room.

"You're supposed to keep an eye on Bloodguard."

"*I am*," she hissed.

"Did you know he's heading for the Elven prince's house?"

Red roses...Wil's attempt to court the elf woman...her tentative acceptance of him...he'll bed her and then be done with her...just like me...just like me....

"Jules!"

"What?"

Tong stared at Jules' livid face. The bitterness transformed her beautiful features into pure ugliness. He watched her struggle to contain her emotions until a frigid calm settled on her face. Tong doubted that it continued below the surface.

THREE

Danyl sat beside Wil and watched the man fine-tune the details of the eastern shoreline, Caldon Island, and the Spice Islands on the map spread out before him. He labeled every inlet, town, village, and waterway. Wil entered the depths and currents in the Strait of Sorrows and all around the islands. He leaned back and rubbed the muscles on his neck and shoulders.

"How can you possibly remember all of that?" asked Danyl.

"Those who do not memorize the hazards are at the bottom of the sea, my friend."

"Are there any other islands or lands beyond Caldon Island?"

"There is an island miles to the east," replied Wil. "Few choose to sail there."

"Why?"

Wil stared at the unfinished corner of the chart. "It is an island about a week's sail to the southeast of Caldon Island. This large chunk of rock is barren except for a few clusters of palm trees, nesting terns, and seals."

"No resources?" questioned Danyl.

Wil closed his eyes and thought back to the hours after the multiple hangings in Daris Haven before it was renamed Graveyard. The wives and children of the men he had hanged cursed his name and spit on him. The spice merchant's family was the worst. Wearing a silk dress and adorned with jewelry, his wife shouted words at him that even he never uttered. Bereft of her station and his money, she feared the retribution of those whom her husband had cheated over the years. And there were many. She quickly realized that he would not fall for her behavior and offered her daughters to him in exchange for their safety. He glanced over at the young girls then shook his head with disgust at their mother. Hatred and conceit radiated from all of their eyes.

28

"You have one hour to pack only what you need," he said to them, then turning to a couple of brigands instructed, "Collect enough things they'll need to survive...fishing hooks and lines, barrels to collect water, blankets, and so forth."

"Why? Where are you sending us?" demanded the spice merchants' wife.

"Forsaken Isle."

"You can't do that! We'll die!"

Wil headed for his office, ignoring the begging and screaming from the square....

"None worth the trip."

"Do you miss the sea, Wil?"

"Sometimes."

"Enough to go back?"

"No."

Danyl and Wil looked up as the new historian entered the library. The elf's short black hair was sprinkled with gray; self-importance exuded from his dark eyes. The pleats on his robes remained evenly spaced even while he walked. He offered the prince a curt nod and ignored Wil before sitting down at his desk. The historian picked up a book from one of several neat stacks and opened it. He tapped his chin with his index finger then placed the book back on top of the others.

Danyl thought of Karolauren, who was brutally murdered during the war with Mahn. Cantankerous and intelligent, Karolauren loved his duties and never stopped searching for even the vaguest answer. The ancient elf's desk had always been littered with books, scrolls, and loose sheets of paper. Karolauren always found whatever he was searching for, regardless of how high the piles were. Danyl missed his mentor and friend.

"You can fill in these areas with the land maps stored in the back," suggested Danyl, pointing to the Rock Lord's realm in the east. "The dwarves provide updates from time to time."

"I need these scrolls," the historian ordered the young apprentice standing near his desk.

The boy took the list and headed toward the shelves.

Danyl studied the historian's pinched features and wondered why his brother had chosen him to fill Karolauren's position. The prince glanced at Wil, who met his gaze and subtly shrugged.

"I'll show you where they are," stated Danyl.

Wil raised a brow for he knew exactly where they were located but followed the elf to the corner of the library.

"Tell me what you think of him," whispered Danyl.

"He's a pompous fool who tries to cover his inabilities with an air of superiority."

"My sentiments exactly."

"He sends the boy to fetch whatever he needs because he has no idea where anything is located in the library," added Wil.

"Father will be evaluating him soon," revealed Danyl.

"What if he fails?"

"Then he will be discharged from his duties."

"Will Styph return to Terracine in search of another historian, Danyl?"

"I don't know. Perhaps someone within Bystyn will be competent enough to fill the station."

"That boy knows the library very well."

"He's only twelve, Wil."

"He's a *smart* twelve."

Danyl smiled and shook his head; Wil slid the maps from their place on the shelf and tucked them under his arm. The friends returned to the table where Styph was studying the incomplete chart.

"Impressive, Wil!"

Wil noticed that Styph and Danyl resembled each other, although Styph was a little taller and broader in the chest than Danyl. There was, however, no mistaking that they were brothers. Wil placed the scrolls on the table.

"Danyl tells me that this is quite the *lively* place," remarked Styph indicating Widows Point.

Wil grinned. "There's something for everyone there. Plenty of gambling houses, restaurants, and, as Danyl found out, ladies to cater to your every whim."

"We should go some time," commented Styph with a wink.

"For the food…maybe."

"Where's your sense of adventure, Danyl?"

"Smashed to bits along Caldon Island's coast."

The trio's laughter earned them an annoyed look from the historian; the boy's face was filled with wonder and curiosity.

"It couldn't have been all bad, Danyl."

"It wasn't if you discount the near drowning and being slammed against sharp boulders by huge waves, the incessant heat, almost being eaten by an enormous shark, dodging the necromancer's fire, and constantly agonizing over whether or not we'd find Ramira and Allad."

"Yet here you are," joked the crown prince.

"Here I'll stay," corrected Danyl with a smirk.

"How about you, Wil? Care to show me around Widows Point some time?"

"I'd gladly show you around the waterfront even though there's a bounty for my head, Styph."

"We'll bring a few of my boys along. Speaking of that, would you two care to join me for some refreshments at the barracks?" inquired Styph.

Danyl grinned, for eating with the guards meant only one thing. "Absolutely!"

Danyl, Styph, and Wil headed down the main avenue; the crown prince's guards followed at a discreet distance. They entered the barracks' dining hall. The guards greeted the trio then made room for them at one of the long wooden tables. Platters of meat, vegetables, cheese, and bread were within easy reach in the middle. One of the elves filled their tankards with ale while everyone else piled food on their plates. The conversations and laughter drifted around the room. Sated, the tables were cleared and the captain of the guard stood and lifted his tankard into the air.

"I propose a toast to all our courageous comrades who sleep in eternity," he began to a silent room. "Especially Nyk, who is truly missed."

Everyone bowed their heads in respect. A moment later the laughter started again.

"Tell me about Nyk," urged Wil.

Everyone immediately quieted down. Wil's sincere interest in the dead prince garnered him more than one appreciative look.

"Our brother was loved and respected by all," began Styph in solemn tones. "He was valiant and understood the intricacies of war. Although he usually wore a serious expression, he was known to indulge in a prank now and then."

"Indeed!" yelled out one of the guards. "Like the time he commanded us to wear dresses and bonnets during one of our patrols!"

"Nyk was the one who first made contact with the Herkahs," explained Danyl. "His men were decimated by the Kreetch on the Broken Plain. He spent weeks in the care of the Herkahs while he recuperated from his injuries. He and Allad became fast friends during their brief time together."

"The first time I encountered the nomads on the plains upon his return from that event I actually thought that Nyk was a Herkah," Drand, Nyk's captain, chimed in. "He wore their clothing and somehow acquired the nomads' fluid movements."

Other guards recounted their memories of the prince, each story filled with great respect for Nyk.

Danyl thought back to the last time he saw Nyk alive. Covered in blood and sweat, his older brother mounted his horse to meet up with Allad and the Elven guard. The brothers exchanged a quick nod before Nyk galloped out of the gate and to his death. No…not death but a lifetime of being occupied and controlled by a vile Vox. Kept imprisoned by Mahn, Ramira was forced to view the possessed elf and Herkah. She freed Nyk by slicing his throat but Mahn prevented her from saving Allad's soul. Thinking back, Danyl realized that that would have been a grave mistake.

"How did your brother die?" asked Wil.

"Honorably," replied Styph in a quiet voice.

Wil glanced questionably at Danyl.

"He was possessed by a Vox," the prince whispered into his ear. "Ramira freed him."

Wil gaped at Danyl. "She killed him?"

"She saved his soul, Wil."

Wil sipped from his tankard while subtly studying both princes and the elves who spoke with great admiration for the dead prince. The brigand began to feel that same sentiment just by listening to those gathered.

"Time to celebrate our brothers!" bellowed Styph while banging his tankard on the table.

A cheer arose from all gathered. One of the elves placed a large glass container on the table; another brought out short glasses.

Wil eyed the dark, round spheres submerged in a liquid filled with unidentifiable bits that floated within. "What are those?"

Styph grinned while unscrewing the top of the vessel. He fished one out and plopped it on the table in front of Wil. Danyl strained some of the liquid into a small glass then pushed it toward Wil. Soon, everyone had a share before them.

"Felsys."

Wil scrutinized the ball. He picked it up and sniffed it: it reeked of garlic, onions, and a potent liquid. "What's a 'Felsys'?"

"A *prominent* part of a mature buck." Styph's understated reply drew more laughter from the elves.

Wil smirked as each elf ate their offering and washed it down with the whiskey. He consumed his then drained his glass to the cheering guards. He squeezed his eyes shut and shuddered; the liquid burned his throat and continued to blaze in his stomach.

"You won't be able to stand yourself in the morning," warned Danyl, who helped himself to another one.

"I take it you won't be sleeping with Ramira tonight?" queried Wil.

"Or maybe tomorrow night, either."

"Tell us a tale from the east, Wil," one of the guards called out.

"Make it worthwhile!" shouted another elf.

Wil downed another glass of whiskey and then leaned back against the chair. Silence invited him to speak.

"We heard rumors of a special place in the northeast corner of Caldon Island. It was supposedly renowned for its *hospitality*. The women were beautiful and the banquets sumptuous. Anyone wishing to partake of all that bounty must pay a hefty price. My men and I collected the required gold and waited at the base of a hill. Torchlight and exotic incense drifted down its sides and covered us in a heady fog. A gorgeous woman wearing a diaphanous gown seemed to float as she walked down the path. She offered us goblets of wine, which we hastily downed. After a few minutes, she escorted us up the wooded path to a most wondrous place. We entered the dining hall where dozens of scantily clad women awaited us. Wine poured out of fountains; fruit and marinated meats were piled onto gold platters. Music soothed our weary souls. Women danced seductively while we reclined upon couches covered in silks. Our instincts became dulled as the night wore on; our *urges* heightened. One by one my men disappeared into the small chambers that extended out from the main hall.

"I suddenly realized that I was alone with one woman. She lay beside me on the couch. Her tanned skin was soft and emitted an enticing scent. Her long blonde hair was silken to the touch. Her deep blue eyes held my gaze. She offered herself to me...."

"And? Did you take her?" demanded one of the elves.

"No, I woke up at the bottom of the hill stripped of all my possessions and covered in my own vomit!"

The elves guffawed.

"We climbed back up the hill but found nothing except our footprints and numerous broken branches!"

"So there was never a hall?" prodded Danyl.

"The drugged wine and incense made us think so," replied Wil with a chuckle. "The Grifters made out well that night!"

Drand handed Wil another Felsys. He slapped him on the back when the pirate devoured it and then drank another glass of whiskey.

"I think that my boys like you, Wil!" remarked Styph.

"The feeling is mutual, Styph."

$\sim$

"Ramira?" Sophie called from the kitchen doorway.

"In here."

Sophie unlatched the bottom half of the door and headed for the front room. Ramira spread a blanket on the floor then added three pillows. Another coverlet remained folded up on the couch. Sophie cocked her head to the side.

"Three fools are eating Felsys," explained Ramira with a smirk.

"This house is going to stink by the morning."

"Three candles, the aromatic oil lamp, and open windows should help. Do you want to stay and help me undress them?"

"I thought you'd never ask," replied Sophie with a smile.

"I don't see the girls that much anymore, Sophie," remarked Ramira while pouring them glasses of wine.

"Cricket and Anci spend a quarter of their time sizing up the right boy, another quarter comparing their choices with their other friends, and a third quarter intentionally ignoring those same boys," laughed Sophie.

"There's still one quarter unaccounted for."

"Um, yes." Sophie sipped from her glass. "That quarter is spent preening for the boys they intend to snub! Didn't you do the same thing when you were their age?"

The kitchen wavered and was replaced with the throne room in Thebes. *Images of the Ceraphine smiting her enemies were painted on the walls behind the golden throne. The Ceraphine wore a conical crown out of beaten gold and a bejeweled necklace that covered most of her chest. Slaves on either side of the Ceraphine waved plumed fans to keep her cool. She stared without blinking at the nobles and other visitors kneeling before her. The Ceraphine gauged the nobles from the surrounding territories and the treasures they each presented for the chance to unite one of their children with hers. Chests overflowing with gold and gems from the south, lumber and furs from the north, and highly prized harbor rights from the west. The Ceraphine signed treaties with them all. Ramira and her siblings became commodities traded to enhance the Ceraphine's influence, wealth, and power. All except for Dar-Ahnet, the next expected Ceraphine. Forced to participate in the Ceraphine's arrogant display of authority, Ramira stood amongst her siblings, bedecked with jewelry and fine linen. Although clothed, she felt naked. And exposed.*

She was traded for lumber rights with the most uncouth individual that the Ceraphine could find. Dar-Ahnet, she remembered, wore a broad smirk when the Ceraphine announced Ramira's pairing. The middle-aged man with poor hygiene habits couldn't wait to bed her. Ramira, however, refused to comply. He grabbed her wrist with one hand and slapped her across the face with the other. Ramira drove her knee into his groin, doubling him over. She brought her fists down on the back of his head and then watched him suck in air through clenched teeth. The Ceraphine's attempt to punish Ramira with the vilest of men backfired on her. Ramira endured the Ceraphine's wrath and was never presented again. The memory dissolved, bringing Ramira back to her home.

"Ramira?"

"I was never one who enjoyed dressing up, Sophie."

"Not even to attract a young man?"

"No."

"So what did you do during those early years?"

"Not very much."

Slurred singing and wild laughter increased in volume as the trio and the guards supporting them ambled toward the kitchen. Ramira and Sophie met them at the door.

"Thank you for bringing them home," Ramira said to the sentries.

"I'll keep all three of them."

The elves nodded and handed them over to the women. They melted into the shadows to guard the crown prince.

Ramira sat Wil and Danyl on the bench by the hearth; Sophie kept them upright by grabbing the backs of their tunics. Wil passed gas; all three of the men chuckled. One by one, Ramira stripped off their clothing, eased them onto the floor, and then covered them with the blanket. She wrinkled her nose when she scooped up the clothes and tossed them in the corner of the yard. No amount of washing could remove the foul stench.

Sophie placed her hands on her hips. "The bearer of the Green Might, a handsome stranger, and the future king of the elves."

Danyl belched, Styph scratched himself, and Wil released another pocket of gas.

"Every woman's dream," Ramira said in a dry tone.

"Bystyn remains in safe hands," Sophie added in a deadpan voice.

Sul-Tak glowered at the constant barricades plaguing their escape from the mountain. Promising escape routes continuously ended in blocked passageways. Impatience beleaguered the Brethren. The demons grew weak with hunger and the exertions of seeking a way out. They would perish if they returned to the cold and ice on the unknown side of the range. That, however, was where the food was. Sul-Tak called all the Brethren together.

"You," he pointed at a group of Vox, "will return to the other side of the mountain and bring food back. Ten Kreetch will continue to find a way back to the land. The rest of us will remain here until the path has been found."

The Kreetch disappeared into the bowels of the mountain. No longer held back by their slower kin, the demons explored any and all possible passages. After three grueling days of searching, only five survived. They emerged leagues apart along the foothills. Exhausted from their ordeal, the demons first order of business was to feed.

~

Seven and Clare rode at the head of the wagons carrying food, drink, and a host of cheerful dwarves. The sun warmed them from a brilliant turquoise sky; the trees to their right glowed with orange, yellow, and red leaves. Deep greens marked the pine trees. The caravan stayed well away from the edge of the woods.

"We'll be in Bystyn in two days, Seven," stated Clare.

"I can't wait to see everyone again."

Seven stuck his hand in his pocket and pulled out a bundle. He unwrapped the material revealing two halves of a hollowed-out stone he had quarried from the heart of Evan's Peak. The pale green color was marbled with fine black and white veins. The dwarf king smiled then stowed Danyl's secret request back into his pocket.

"What have you got there?"

"Nothing," replied Seven.

"'Nothing' indeed," said Clare shaking her head.

"Wyl is what…four months old now?"

Clare nodded and then started laugh.

"What's so funny?"

"Wil acting as mid-wife. I somehow doubt that he volunteered."

"Ramira probably held one of her knives to his throat," chuckled Seven.

"Well, there's nothing more intimidating than a woman in the throes of childbirth," declared the dwarf queen with a smirk.

"Especially if that woman is Ramira!"

~

Starvation weakened the Kreetch's ability to capture the animals that scurried away from its presence. The demon moved toward the plains in search of anything to eat. It finally managed to seize an unsuspecting rabbit. Sound traveled to where it ripped into its meal.

The Kreetch crept to the forest's perimeter and beheld the dwarves with a gleeful anticipation. Its instincts urged it to rush forward and feast on the humans. The Kreetch dashed out onto the plains, its maniacal shrieks announcing its presence.

The dwarves flinched at the all too familiar sound. It didn't take long to see the demon bounding toward them from the tree line. The dwarves grabbed their swords and scanned the edge of the woods for more of the despicable demons. It half-ran, half-scrabbled in the dwarves' direction, occasionally collapsing then getting up once more. Foam covered its chin and chest.

"Keep an eye out for any more of them!" shouted Seven.

The king noted that the Kreetch fell often, dragging itself for several yards before managing to get to its feet and resuming its attack. Its mouth remained open; its chest heaved. Was the demon rabid?

Seven motioned the dwarves away from the demon then hacked it in two when it launched itself at him with the last of its strength. No other Kreetch emerged from the forest.

"This is a bad sign," muttered the king.

He motioned for them to speed up and assigned armed dwarves on either side of the wagons. They constantly watched the woods, their swords at the ready.

"Why was there just one, Seven?" asked Clare.

"I don't know, but it was in very bad shape."

"When will we *finally* be rid of those dreadful things?"

When indeed? he thought.

~

Wil held the single red rose up to his nose and inhaled its perfume. Smiling, he headed toward the tavern. He intended to ask Hanna to dinner. He halted at the end of the alleyway and watched Hanna and an elf walk out of the inn and in the direction of the square. His arm was draped across her shoulder; hers encircled his waist. They shared a laugh then he kissed her cheek.

Wil looked down at the rose and sighed. She should have told him that there was someone else. He waited until the couple was out of sight and then walked over to his usual table. He placed the rose on it, stuffed his hands in his trouser pockets, and then headed for Danyl's and Ramira's home. He entered the kitchen and was immediately met by Blue, who insisted that he dote on her.

"Hello, beautiful! You too, Ramira."

"Charming as ever," she chided him affably.

Kayla crawled over to him. He lifted her high into the air then hugged her.

"Well? Did you ask her?"

"No," he hid his disappointment.

"Why not?" persisted Ramira.

"Because she had another escort."

"I thought she was beginning to tolerate you?"

"As did I," he replied, kissing Kayla on the cheek.

Ramira noted the barely concealed hurt in his eyes. Hanna was a good match for him and he really seemed to like her. Wil needed a woman like Hanna, whose inner strength and intelligence would complement Wil's personality. Ramira placed another setting on the table just as Danyl walked in.

Upon seeing him, Kayla reached for her father. Danyl gathered his daughter up in his arms. "Father says we have three days to ourselves, Wil."

Wil had planned to spend most of those three days with Hanna.

"Why so glum?" asked the elf.

"I wanted to finish those last few additions to the chart," he lied.

Danyl looked questionably at Ramira who mouthed, *He saw Hanna with someone else.*

"The dwarves and the Herkahs will be arriving soon," stated Danyl while spooning food into Kayla's mouth. "Perhaps we can convince Seven and Allad to join us for another round of Felsys."

Ramira grimaced. "I don't know how you can eat that!"

"Have you ever tried it?"

40

"No, Wil, I haven't. Just smelling it on him," she pointed at Danyl, "is enough for me!"

"And to think Seven ate thirteen Felsys," remarked Wil, helping himself to more cheese and slices of meat. "Poor Clare."

"She banished him to the stables," chuckled Danyl. "Even the horses objected to his presence."

"I doubt that your father would insult the dwarven king by leaving him in the barn."

"Clare insisted and everyone silently thanked her for doing so," clarified the prince.

"How did Seven react when he was finally allowed back into the castle?"

"He wore his exile like a badge of honor!"

"Seven will undoubtedly entertain us with that story, too," warned Ramira.

The men watched Ramira pick up her crying baby and carry him to the sofa to nurse. Danyl turned his attention back to Kayla, who giggled when he wiped the porridge from her face and hands. Wil laughed when the abrupt concentration on her face was followed by an unmistakable odor.

"I'll be right back," muttered Danyl.

Wil sat down beside Ramira and smiled as his son's tiny fingers wrapped around one of his. He gently caressed Wyl's hand with his thumb; happiness emanated from his face. Wyl's eyes closed as sleep fulfilled the only other need a baby had at that age.

"What are you thinking?" Ramira asked.

"What a great mother you are and how fortunate I am to be a part of this."

Ramira kissed his cheek and then carried her sleeping son upstairs; Wil and Danyl cleared the table and washed the dishes.

Hanna waved good-bye to her companion and was about to enter the tavern when she spotted the rose. She picked it up and searched for Wil. She glanced at her companion's retreating back then at the rose once more. Hanna shook her head and marched over to Ramira's and Danyl's house.

Danyl, Ramira, and Wil sat together after the children were left to nap. They shared glasses of wine and small talk. A familiar voice called out to them. Wil's face wilted for a moment before regaining his composure.

"Come in, Hanna," Ramira invited.

"Thank you, Ramira. I don't mean to intrude, but I really need to speak to *him*," she pointed at Wil.

"Danyl and I will give you some privacy."

"That won't be necessary," she informed them.

Wil collected his emotions.

"You left this," she held up the rose, "without speaking to me?"

"You were with someone," he mumbled.

"Did it ever occur to you to ask who the other man was? No, of course not," she interjected. "It's much easier to wallow in your self-pity."

Danyl crossed his arms and stared at the floor; Ramira could barely keep from laughing at the flabbergasted look on Wil's face.

"Well?" demanded Hanna.

Wil looked up at the ceiling. "Who was the man escorting you today?"

"My brother."

"'Brother'?" Wil's face paled then flushed.

Danyl covered his eyes with his hand and quietly chuckled.

"Yes, you fool! I was looking for you so that I could introduce the two of you."

Oh, Pirate…don't let this woman go!

"Umm…."

"I happen to find you somewhat interesting and expect you to escort me to dinner the day after tomorrow."

"Umm…"

Hanna stuck her index finger into his chest. "I'll be ready at six...d*on't* be late."

Wil stared at her; the silence in the room was broken by Ramira's muffled giggles.

Hanna turned her back to Wil then winked at the couple before leaving.

"I'm glad that I amuse you two," he growled. "She finds me 'somewhat interesting'," he said pointing at Hanna's retreating form. "This one," he indicated Ramira, "says that I'm 'just adequate', and one woman tried to kill me!"

"Only one?" Ramira's incredulous tone echoed in the kitchen.

"All right...several tried, but one almost succeeded. *You* only *thought* about slaying me, so *you* don't count."

"Actually, I was tempted to kill you on several occasions."

Wil placed his hands on his hips. "Let's see: In my office back in Graveyard."

"That's one," she acknowledged.

"After you defeated Doomah." He avoided the topic of offering her a king's ransom to sleep with him.

"That's two."

"When I confessed to you."

"That's three."

Ramira, he noted, waited for him to add more incidents. Wil pursed his lips in thought. "That's all I can think of."

"Don't worry, Pirate," she said. "I'll wager that you'll do or say something that will extend that list."

Grumbling under his breath, Wil huffed out of the house.

Danyl smiled then held Ramira. "Any more nightmares?"

She shook her head.

"We should talk with Zada when she gets here."

Ramira nodded. She needed Zada's counsel on more than just her nightmare.

~

The nomads breathed a collective sigh of relief when an Elven patrol rode up to them. After exchanging greetings, Allad sent two nomads along with a pair of elves in advance of the rest of the tribe.

"We should be in Bystyn by nightfall," updated Allad.

"I can't wait to see everyone…especially the new baby," said Zada.

"A bright spot considering the news we bear."

Zada slipped her hand into the pouch hanging from her belt and pulled out a small glass vial. She tilted her head to one side and wondered why Danyl requested a few grains of sand from the heart of the Great White Desert. She deposited it back into the pouch and shoved the mysterious request to the back of her mind.

The sun hung low on the horizon when the nomads made camp along the western wall of the city. Allad and Zada continued up the avenue, smiling and waving at the elves along the way. They dismounted in front of the castle where the king waited to welcome them. Alyxandyr invited them to refresh themselves before ushering them into his study.

"The dwarves are expected within the next few days," stated the king.

"These halls are too quiet without Seven!" joked Allad.

"Any news that you'd like to share?" asked the king.

"Nothing that can't wait for when the dwarves arrive," answered Zada.

Danyl and Ramira carried their children into the castle. Kayla giggled and pointed at the guards and staff, who couldn't help but smile at the little bundle of energy in the prince's arms. Wyl slept within the shawl draped across Ramira's shoulder. They followed the king's personal aide to the dining room and beamed when they beheld the Herkahs. They embraced each other. Kayla stared at the nomads for a moment then hid her face against Danyl's neck. She squirmed in her father's arms when she heard her grandfather's voice.

"She's adorable," remarked Zada.

Zada noted the faint tendrils of amethyst and emerald surrounding Kayla. *Will you inherit your parents' magic or will your baby brother?*

"Come here my little girl!" Alyxandyr called, taking the child into his arms. Kayla's kisses lit up Alyxandyr's face with joy.

Ramira unwrapped the shawl and presented Wyl to the Herkah couple. The baby opened his eyes.

Allad stared into the azure sea around Caldon Island; Zada ran her index finger across Wyl's petal soft cheek and noted that his ears were rounded like Ramira's but that his brows arched upward.

Zada perceived an unfamiliar yet benign silver wisp rising up from the baby that floated beside the amethyst haze. Its unexpected presence mystified her.

The group gathered together in the adjoining sitting room after dinner. They looked up as Wil entered and warmly greeted everyone.

"Glad to see you made it," greeted Alyx. "You've never met Zada, have you?"

Wil offered the nomad a respectful nod. Her understated refinement was blended with an air of mystery. "It's an honor to meet you."

Zada's inner sight opened, revealing a fleeting silver wisp around the man. Confusion morphed into disbelief as the truth worked its way into her mind. The Herkah hid her shock before anyone noticed.

"Allad," Wil stuck out his hand, "it's good to see you again."

"Likewise, Wil."

"I've put him to good use," stated Alyx pointing at Wil. "He has excellent recollection skills and has been charting the waters off the land to the east."

"It was either that or cleaning out the stables," teased Danyl.

"He certainly is quite adept at shoveling manure," added Ramira.

Laughter prompted Wil to hold his hands up in mock defeat.

Danyl walked up to Wil and placed his hand on the man's shoulder. "Wil also participated in a deep-rooted Elven guard tradition."

"Felsys," nodded Allad. "How many did you eat, Wil?"

"I stopped counting at five."

"You couldn't count after five," clarified Danyl.

Keeping her thoughts veiled, Zada studied the interaction between Wil, Danyl, and Ramira. She, of course, focused her attention on her children. Wil and Danyl acted as if they had been friends for many years. Either Danyl was unaware that Wil fathered the boy or he had come to terms with that fact. Zada speculated that it was probably the latter. What, however, would have prompted Ramira to sleep with Wil?

Kayla curled up against Blue on the sofa; the cat watched everything with half-lidded eyes. Ramira picked Wyl up and rubbed his back until he drifted off to sleep. Kissing his head, she thought of Zaura. The wraith gave so much to keep Wil safe, including her own life. Ramira was glad that he reconnected with his mother's love, even though it meant experiencing a harsh and painful point in his life. She sighed inwardly, for she was the only one who knew the truth about Wil and the other wraiths.

Ramira sat down beside her daughter and brushed the strands of auburn hair from her face. Kayla's legacy will be shared with her once she is old enough to understand it. Wyl was another story. Should they tell him or continue pretending that Danyl was his father? How would he react knowing the truth behind his birth? Would he accept it or turn away from all of them? Ramira intended to discuss all of this with Danyl, but first she needed a woman's ear.

Zada watched Ramira. The most powerful demon in the land tended to her babies with complete love and devotion. It was difficult to imagine her as the Black Queen who defeated the wraith and nearly climbed out of Doth-Khan to destroy them all. Only one man prevented that from happening.

Zada glanced at Wil, who shared a laugh with the others. The man was at ease with his companions. The bond of friendship between them was unmistakable. Her inner sight clicked on revealing the emerald aura and the faint silver glow in apparent harmony. Did Wil have some form of magic?

Zada's attention shifted to an approaching Ramira. "Motherhood suits you well, Ramira."

"Everything that I've ever wanted is here, Zada."

"Imhap, Horemb, and Oma would be proud."

"I owe everything to them," she replied in a reverent tone.

"We all do."

Ramira looked into Zada's eyes. "I need some guidance."

"Walk with me."

They stopped at the end of the hallway and sat on the deep sill. A refreshing breeze drifted in through the window overlooking the garden. A full moon rose in the sky; crickets and night birds provided the evening music. Zada patiently waited for Ramira to gather her thoughts.

"I had a terrible nightmare, Zada. The Ankh-Nam tried to infuse itself into me again."

"That's because it is no longer in Doth-Khan."

"Where is it?" whispered Ramira in a fearful voice.

"It lingers beyond my inner sight," replied the nomad. "Like the Brethren."

"We can only hope that they are all gone forever."

"A wonderful thought, Ramira, but unlikely."

Ramira remained quiet for a while, her gaze never leaving her intertwined fingers.

"There's something else on your mind."

Ramira took a deep breath. "Three wraiths accompanied Suh to his enclosure. One of them, Zulant whom you knew as Abby, decided to betray her two sisters. The necromancer used Zistak for her blood and the other sister, Zaura, ran away when she sensed Zulant's treachery. Zulant was bound to the island as long as her sisters lived. Suh bled Zistak to death and Zulant never located Zaura, who must have died or else Zulant wouldn't have been able to come here."

Intrigued, Zada crossed her arms and leaned against the window

47

sill.

"Zaura managed to hide from them for many years and eventually gave birth to a son, who she shielded from his wraith heritage. He grew up and took his revenge on the men who ultimately killed his mother. He, in turn, was overthrown by Suh."

"Captain Wil Bloodguard is part wraith?" murmured a stunned Zada. The origin of the silver tendril suddenly made sense.

"Yes," confirmed Ramira.

"Does he know about his legacy?"

"No, and this is where it becomes complicated."

Zada patiently waited for Ramira to acknowledge what her inner sight had already discerned.

"Wil is the father of my son."

The Herkah subtly nodded. "I know, Ramira."

"How?"

"My inner sight divulged that to me," began the nomad, "but what confounds me is *how* that happened."

"We were both under the influence of a potion, Zada."

"Suh?"

"Fate."

Laughter and conversation drifted into the hallway when an elf carrying a tray of food opened the door to the room.

"Am I to assume that only the four of us know the truth, Ramira?"

"About Wil fathering my son, yes."

"Have you told Danyl about Wil's heritage?"

"Not yet."

"What happened in Doth-Khan, Ramira?" asked Zada after a long silence.

Ramira closed her eyes and relived that terrible time. "I placed the Ankh-Nam around my neck and immediately felt the frigid magic surge through me. It seduced me with promises of eternal life and ruling unopposed. I heeded its promises so that I could defeat Zulant. The Black Queen triumphed and turned to eradicate her last foe."

"You."

"Yes," admitted Ramira.

"Did the Black Queen feel threatened?"

"There had to be a complete transformation, Zada, and I was on the cusp of being powerless to stop it. My soul was driven…no beaten down into the farthest recesses of my being. I was drowning in a sea of malevolence."

"What happened?"

"For a brief moment I surfaced and was able to see Wil's terrified face before I was yanked back down into the darkness. It was there that I discovered Wyl. I wielded the Source of Darkness to protect my unborn son and to destroy the Black Queen. I would not have survived otherwise, Zada."

The nomad mulled over Ramira's words and then thought back to Suh. His abduction of Ramira and Allad had set into motion a set of circumstances that culminated in their present situation. Ramira was able to extinguish the parasitic Vox that possessed Allad without killing her mate. The necromancer's attack on Graveyard and Wil's subsequent imprisonment forced Wil to reevaluate his life. It was Wil's commitment to Ramira that gave him the courage to not only enter Doth-Khan but to face the Black Queen. Had he faltered or not ridden after Ramira and Allad, she believed, none of them would be alive. She also remembered the Green Might's blistering attack on Ramira when they returned from Doth-Khan. The Elven magic recognized that Ramira's unborn child was not Danyls. The question was, to what end would these events lead? Zada thought back to the war against Mahn. Hopefully this conclusion would be less devastating.

Zada took Ramira's hands in hers. "Everything will sort itself out in the end, Ramira."

FOUR

Relief flooded the dwarves' faces when they espied Bystyn in the distance. They waved to an Elven patrol, half of which rode back to the city while the others accompanied the dwarves. The dwarves did not encounter any more demons along the way, but that did nothing to alleviate their fears. One meant that there were surely more…but where?

The dwarf couple entered the city and headed straight for the castle. The reunion with the other leaders was conducted in Alyx's chambers after the king and queen washed off some of the road dirt. Seven's normally jovial mood was tempered by something that worried the others.

"It's good to see you again, my friends," said Alyx.

Mason, Styph, Zada, Allad, and Danyl embraced the dwarf couple.

"That almost didn't happen," replied Seven. "We encountered a Kreetch a few days east of here."

"Was anyone hurt?" asked the alarmed Elven king.

"No," replied Clare. "The demon was exhausted and easily killed."

"Didn't the Brethren get trapped when Doth-Khan collapsed, Allad?"

"Yes, but they might have been forced into the myriad of tunnels that branch outward from the demon lair," explained the Herkah.

"Fetch Wil and Ramira," the Elven king ordered one of the guards by the door.

"If one found a way back into the land then the others might follow," cautioned Mason.

"It's been about a year since the demon lair was destroyed," stated Allad. "The Brethren have been on the move since then and could be anywhere."

The door opened and admitted Wil, who had been working in the library.

"You summoned me, Alyx?"

The Elven king waved him to a seat and repeated what had befallen the dwarves.

"You and Ramira were the last to be in Doth-Khan, Wil," began Zada. "Did you notice where the demons went before the desert buried it?"

"There were countless tunnels that diverged off in a....," he pressed his lips together in thought, "north, northeasterly direction."

"Do the passageways loop around back to the demon lair?"

"They cannot return to Doth-Khan, Alyx," explained Zada, "because it was completely flattened shortly before we left to come here."

"Are there tunnels that run through those mountains like there are in the range abutting the desert, Allad?" inquired Seven.

"The range to the north is an impregnable barrier," clarified Mason.

"But what if there *are* ways through those mountains as well?" persisted the dwarf king.

"Nothing has ever passed through that range," disclosed the Elven king. His uncertainty, however, started to cloud his mind.

"Father," Styph piped in, "what of the outlaws living in the caves between here and Evan's Peak? Their hideouts are within the mountains."

Alyxandyr had forgotten about them. He looked at Seven.

"From what we know, the outlaws inhabit a series of caves," answered the dwarf king. "I'm not sure about their configurations."

The guard opened the door for Ramira. Wyl lay in the shawl around her shoulders; Kayla was in her arms.

Seven and Clare couldn't contain themselves. They walked over to the children and spent several minutes fussing over them while the Elven king updated Ramira on the situation.

"Can you add anything to this, Ramira?" asked the king.

Ramira knew what he asked of her. She glanced over at Danyl, who subtly nodded.

"I had a nightmare not too long ago," she confessed.

"What kind of nightmare?" questioned the Elven king.

Zada quietly listened to Ramira repeat some of their conversation.

"The amulet tried to infuse itself into me again," she replied while absently touching the scar through her tunic.

"Was that the only time you dreamt of that?" Mason asked.

"Yes."

"The Ankh-Nam has not been destroyed," commented Zada. "It still seeks you, Ramira."

"Which means the Brethren are still alive and roaming around somewhere," added Mason.

"And they will return for their queen." Zada's words punctuated the chamber.

Ramira shuddered with revulsion. The very idea of meeting up with the demons again left her feeling cold inside. She could well imagine the seething hatred they had for her because she had rejected them. Ush-Tak retained some measure of intelligence, which is why he brought the Ankh-Nam to her for safekeeping and out of Zulant's hands. What of the Vox who now led the Brethren? What motivated him? Regardless of who commanded the demons, they had little choice but to find her. She was their queen. Only she could brandish the Black Queen's might. They would utilize anything in their power to either coerce her to accept her place amongst them or destroy everything dear to her.

"Ramira?"

The Elven king's voice brought her back to the present. "I believe Zada is correct, Alyx."

The Elven king nodded. He locked gazes with Allad and then Seven. "We'll send out patrols to keep an eye out for the demons. With any luck, the one that confronted you, Seven, is the exception."

～

Two Kreetch emerged from the mountain a short distance from each other. Like its kin that the dwarves killed, both were weak with hunger. The demons approached each other, their instincts to survive blinding them. Snarling, they collected the last of their strength and charged. The violent contact sent them spinning across the ground. They tore at each other until the grass was smeared with their blood. Whimpering with pain, the debilitated winner of the contest slumped onto the carcass and ceased moving.

~

Wil headed up the stairs and then stopped in front of Hanna's rooms. He straightened out his tunic, ran his fingers through his hair, took a deep breath, and then knocked on her door. He heard footsteps then offered her a smile when she opened it.

"I'm on time."

Hanna smiled and grabbed a light shawl before locking the door behind her. She took his arm when they exited the building. Lanterns were strung along the streets and adorned the square where others milled about. A full moon rose in the inky night sky; stars glittered overhead. The early evening was comfortable even with a faint touch of autumn in the air. Hanna placed her wrap loosely around her shoulders. They stopped at a tavern fronting the square; laughter and conversation spilled out through the partially open windows.

Jules had watched Wil and Hanna leave the building from within the shadowy alleyway. Keeping to the shadows, Jules followed them to an inn a couple of streets over. She'd seen Wil adjust the woman's shawl then offer her his arm. The woman had whispered something in his ear; he'd smiled in return. His actions were a little awkward, Jules thought, but the tenderness with which he completed them was not. Jules' mouth was a tight line; resentment glittered in her eyes.

Wil held the door open for Hanna. The headwaiter led them out to the patio and to a table for two. Even though most of the tables were occupied with diners, the arrangement of the potted plants offered everyone some privacy. A bottle of wine, bread basket, and a covered platter were placed on the table moments later. Wil and Hanna ordered their meals. The elf lifted up the dome and set cups of butternut squash soup in front of the couple.

"When was the last time that *you* were served?"

They each helped themselves to the warm bread.

"It's been a long time," she replied while smearing butter on her slice.

Jules snuck back around and eased her way near their table. She hid between the bushes and the building abutting the patio and listened to their conversation.

"So," began Wil, "other than your brother, do you have any other family?"

"A sister. She's as mean and useless as her drunken mate."

"I take it that you two don't speak?"

"Not since that fool tried to have his way with me during one of his inebriated moments," she stated sourly. "She accused me of trying to seduce him then demanded that I leave and never come back."

"There's no chance of mending that rift?"

"I tried several times, but his influence over her is too strong. She'd rather accept him than face the truth."

Wil discerned the constrained sadness in her voice. The silence between them lasted for a few moments while she wrestled with her feelings.

"How about you? Any family?"

"No."

"What about your mother and father?"

"My mother was murdered when I was ten and I killed my father years later."

Hanna studied his face, which reflected both sorrow and a simmering hatred. The tone of his voice was direct; the look in his eyes unapologetic.

"Why did you slay him?" she quietly asked.

"Because he hurt my mother."

"Do you regret it?"

"No."

The server brought them their meals. Neither one noticed the slight rustling sound from beyond the potted foliage.

"What did you do for a living?"

Hanna scooped roasted vegetables and spicy venison chunks onto her plate. Wil filled his dish and then reached for another slice of bread.

"I was a businessman on Caldon Island," he said. *Pirate…*he suppressed a smile when Ramira's voice echoed in his mind.

"What kind of business?" she asked.

"My ships ran spices, precious metals and gems, or whatever else was in demand from the island to the mainland."

"Was it profitable?"

"Yes."

"Did *you* ever sail back and forth across the sea?"

"Many times."

"What was it like? Being on the sea?" she inquired.

There was a detached look in his eyes as he spoke. "The sea is a temperamental mistress. You can count every star reflected off her surface one moment and then be smashed to bits within her devastating embrace the next. The wind tugs at your hair and clothes while you listen to the whoosh of the waves. The deck rises and falls below your feet, granting you a sense of freedom that few can truly appreciate."

"Spoken like a man in love."

"I always respected her, Hanna."

"Did she ever try to kill you?"

"I have yet to find one woman who hasn't tried to kill me," he said, wearing a lop-sided grin.

"So why abandon everything and venture to Bystyn?"

"I lost everything to a man who attacked my town and imprisoned me for over a year. I escaped and, since I had nowhere else to go, headed west until I came upon Bystyn."

Hanna studied Wil's face. Conflicting emotions flowed across his features. "That explanation is about as thorough as saying that the city is constructed of gray stones."

Wil looked into his glass; moonlight reflected off the red wine. "It would take more than one dinner to explain it all," he replied in a subdued voice.

"I might be interested in another meal."

"You wouldn't believe half of what I could tell you."

Hanna drained her glass and nodded at Wil to pour her more wine. They remained silent when the server removed their dishes and brought another bottle.

"I have a question for you, Wil."

"Ask it."

"Why me?"

"What do you mean?"

"This city is full of beautiful women who would do anything to be with you so, why choose me?"

Hanna's question forced Wil to revisit his past relationships. All revolved around his physical needs, including the one he had with Jules. She deluded him into thinking that…that what? That she loved him? There was never a bond between them. The only woman he ever connected with was Ramira. It was Ramira who reconnected him with his mother's wisdom and love, sentiments he had forsaken while forging ahead with his revenge. He was drawn to Hanna's no-nonsense attitude and wit. She was an attractive woman who was unafraid to speak her mind. Wil looked into Hanna's eyes.

"Because," he said taking her hands in his, "you're the first woman to tell me that I'm 'somewhat interesting'."

Hanna started to laugh; Wil joined in.

A slow, wicked grin spread across Jules' face. She knew Wil spoke the truth, but he left out a great many details. Jules was more than willing to flesh out some of them for the elf woman. Or twist them enough to plant the seeds of doubt in the woman's mind.

"And you? Why do you put up with my pursuing you?"

"You always leave a generous tip."

They finished their meal and left the tavern, trailed by an indistinguishable figure scrutinizing their every move. They strolled around the decorated square side by side, bathed in the golden lamp light.

Hanna thought back to his confession. Wil's emotions ran deep and were kept well hidden. He displayed intelligence, humor, and a suggestive mischievousness; what dwelled in his heart, however, remained elusive. Hanna noticed the intrigued looks some of the passersby gave them and smiled inwardly.

"Would you like to sit for a while?" he asked.

Hanna nodded then pointed to a bench situated beneath an arbor at the edge of the park. Wil, she noted, casually scanned the crowd.

"Tell me something about you that no one else knows, Wil."

He shifted his gaze from the bustling square to her. "I'm glad that Suh destroyed my town and kept me a prisoner."

"Why?"

"Because what I lost paled in comparison to what I gained."

"And that is?"

"A new life," he stated quietly while reliving the moment his son was born.

Tenderness and contentment surfaced on his face for a moment. He veiled his emotions and offered her a slightly embarrassed grin. "And you? What are you hiding?" he inquired.

"I crave excitement."

"What kind of 'excitement' are you referring to?"

She shrugged. "Fast-paced and dangerous, yet something meaningful."

"An adventure?"

"Something like that," she laughed.

"Those don't always end the way you want them to, Hanna."

"It's what happens *during* the journey that counts, Wil, and not always how it ends."

Wil thought of the trek west to Doth-Khan. His intention was to atone for what he had done to Ramira, but he could never have imagined that meant facing the Black Queen in the demon lair. Luckily for everyone, that 'adventure' ended well.

"It's getting late and I have a long day tomorrow."

Wil escorted Hanna back to her home. Standing before her open door, he felt awkward and unsure of what to do.

"I enjoyed your company tonight, Wil."

"Would you consider joining me for another dinner?"

"I might. Goodnight, Wil."

Hanna unexpectedly closed the door. Wil stood there for a moment wearing a befuddled look on his face. Unsure of how to process her abrupt retreat, he headed to his room. Wil undressed and flopped down on his bed. Unused to being dismissed by a woman, he stared at the ceiling looking for answers. He never dined with the women in Graveyard, not even Jules. He and his eager partner spent time in bed and then his companion would leave. Hanna could have invited him in for a glass of wine or at least given him a kiss on the cheek. What did she think he was going to do? What was he supposed to do?

~

Cloaked and hooded against the chilly night, Zordana walked unseen past the guards stationed at the gate and up the main thoroughfare. Except for the nightly patrols, she was the only one about. She halted in the center of the square and opened her mind. An invisible crackling heat prompted her to turn right and stand before a house. Wary of drawing attention to herself, the wraith cautiously probed the magic from within the shadows. To her surprise, she noted two other powers. They, too, began to stir. Zordana tapped her index finger to her thin lips. *Three powers? In one place? No wonder Suh can't stay away!*

The wraith spotted a pair of luminescent green eyes in the second story window. Zordana took a few steps to the right. The eyes followed her. She ambled to the left with the same results. Rare was the creature that could identify a wraith. *What are you?*

~

Ramira's dreamless sleep parted, revealing the ancient city of Thebes. It stood proud beneath the late afternoon sky. Water flowed from the fountains lining the main avenue to the palace. Protected beneath squat palms, flowering shrubs sat nestled between the founts. No birds flew amongst the branches; no dogs roamed the street. Ramira looked around. She was alone. A dry wind stirred her nearly transparent linen gown; finely crafted gold chains hung from her diadem.

Ramira walked up the stone steps and into the cool confines of the palace. No sentries patrolled the hallways nor did she see any scribes rushing to their assigned duties with armfuls of scrolls. Footsteps echoed in Imhap's chamber. Ramira hastened toward the room and pushed open the gilded door. The chamber was empty. She was about to leave when the breeze pushed a rolled-up scroll in her direction. It stopped at her feet. Ramira picked it up and unrolled it. It was blank. She unfurled every scroll she could find with the same results. Ramira ran back outside and stared at the columns: none were adorned with pictures or writing.

The setting sun painted the white granite walls with shades of apricot, red, lavender, and smoky blues. The sky darkened; the full moon rose. The fountains erupted with fire that illuminated the road to the palace. Ramira shivered with unease as the ghostly ruins shimmered once then disappeared...

The Green Might jolted Danyl into wakefulness. The elf sat up in bed, the eerie sensation that someone was in the house compelling him to investigate. He glanced down at Ramira, who softly moaned in her sleep, before checking on Kayla and Wyl. The children slept soundly, but Blue stared unblinkingly out the window.

"What's out there, Blue?"

A low growl rattled in her throat; her ears twitched.

Danyl dressed and headed for the door; Blue prevented him from going downstairs. The cat's tail flicked back and forth while her gaze was locked onto his. Danyl felt an involuntary shiver run up his spine.

Ramira sat up in bed and glanced at the rumpled blankets, the indentation left by his body was still warm to the touch. She could hear Blue's muted snarl in the children's room. She dashed out of bed and called out to the elf in a panicky voice.

"Danyl?"

Blue held his attention for a moment more and then returned to the window.

Ramira touched his arm, startling him. "Danyl? What's wrong?"

"I thought I heard something."

Ramira looked at Blue, who stared out into the night. The cat was normally calm and had only acted this way one other time: the night Kayla was born. Because Abby was there.

"Blue despises wraiths," she murmured.

Danyl looked from Ramira to Blue. The cat continued to search the darkness for her elusive prey.

"First Abby and now the possibility of another one of those wretched beings roaming around the land," muttered Ramira. The last thing she wanted was to confront another Zulant, especially without the Ankh-Nam to grant her that extra power.

"I wonder what *this* one wants." Danyl's sarcastic tone filled the room.

"Zistak and Zaura weren't evil," whispered Ramira more to herself, "maybe this one isn't, either."

"Who are they?"

Ramira silently chastised herself for speaking out loud. "What?"

"Zistak and Zaura…who are they?"

"Zistak was the wraith Suh kept imprisoned for her blood."

"And Zaura?"

"Wil's mother."

Danyl stared at her for a long time. His mouth opened then closed without ever saying a single word. Wil's revelation about his past flooded into the elf's mind. His mother chose to raise him as a normal child and did not reveal his heritage to protect him. How different would things now be if he had known about his birthright?

"Does Wil know?"

Ramira shook her head. "You're not angry?"

"I'm an elf who bears the Green Might and who is forever beholden to a thousand-year-old demon who wields her own brand of magic." He took her hands into his. "We have two children by two different fathers. Our children, by the way, are guarded by a huge cat who thinks they are her kittens. I've battled demons and gone back in time with a ghost and a Herkah. So, the fact that our son is one-half demon, one-quarter man, and one-quarter wraith somehow does not surprise me."

Wyl began to fuss. Ramira picked him up, sat on the short sofa by the window, and nursed him. Danyl seated himself beside her and caressed the baby's cheek.

"Wil told you what happened to his mother, didn't he?" Ramira asked quietly.

"Yes."

"Tell me."

Danyl disclosed Wil's heartbreaking account of his childhood that influenced the rest of his years. The truth about his mother clarified Wil's attitude and decisions over the course of his life.

Ramira kissed Wyl then gently placed her son back in his bed while she continued to listen to Danyl.

"You're going to have to tell him, Ramira."

"Perhaps he - like me - was meant to find out the truth on his own."

"You are the mother of his child." He lifted her chin until she looked into his eyes. "You have an obligation to tell him."

He kissed her then gathered her in his arms.

Hanna cleared the last of the tables, her mind preoccupied with Wil. She found it curious that a man who was used to wealth and power would accept a simple life so far from home. His love of the sea was obvious; his business expertise lucrative. *I'm glad that Suh destroyed my town and kept me a prisoner,* echoed in her mind. What could possibly replace everything that he lost? *A new life.*

A boy with shaggy hair and a dirty face broke through her reverie. He stood as if waiting for her to acknowledge him.

"Can I help you?"

The boy hesitantly advanced.

"I won't bite you."

"I…I don't mean to bother you," said Jules in a pitiable voice.

"What do you want?"

"Um…the man you were with last night…."

"What about him?"

"I know him."

Hanna waited for the boy to continue. "What about him?"

"He's a pirate and a murderer. He used to raid and pillage a lot of the ports on Caldon Island."

"How do you know this?" asked Hanna.

"I was his cabin boy for three years."

"And?"

"He did…he did…" Jules nervously fumbled with the hem of her tunic, "…terrible things to me."

An unbidden uneasiness began to form in Hanna's mind while she listened to the boy's restrained account.

Jules carefully devised the rest of her story. "The trip to the island was only two days but he could never *wait.*"

Hanna's face was unreadable; she listened to the barely concealed distress in the boy's voice. She watched the boy rub the scars around his wrists.

Jules fingered the welts she had inflicted last night. The redness was gone but the ridges remained. "He only cares about himself."

"Why are you telling me this?" inquired Hanna in a quiet voice.

"Because I don't want you to get hurt like I did."

"Why are you here then?" probed Hanna, suspicion echoing in her mind.

"I wanted to get as far away from him as possible. If I'd known he was here, I would have gone elsewhere."

"What will he do to you if he finds you?"

"Please don't tell him about me or what I told you." Jules played her final card, "I don't want him to kill me, too."

Jules fled down the nearest alley and then peered around the corner. The elf woman stood there for a while before resuming her chores.

"That'll give you something to think about!"

FIVE

Suh eyed the large inn in the fading light as they rounded the Dragon's Backbone. The series of protruding boulders ran in a straight line for almost thirty yards. The U-shaped wooden structure, barns, and sheds occupied most of the clearing. Several men sat in chairs along the porch; some propped their feet on the railing while others leaned against the wall.

Suh dismounted, handed the reins of his horse to one of the brigands, and then walked up the splintered steps. He ignored the men and entered the building. Round tables filled the main room; a staircase on the right led to the second floor. A wooden bar took up most of the back wall. He glanced at his reflection in the mirror hanging behind it then searched for the proprietor. A thin woman with a gray ponytail approached him.

She studied the necromancer. "I'm Warren. How may I be of service?"

Suh noted the calculating look in Warren's eyes. "Are you the owner?"

She offered the necromancer a forced smile. "Indeed I am."

"Would you have lodging for thirty men?"

A stranger riding with thirty men was unusual. The thieves, murderers, and thugs who came and went usually traveled in groups of six or less. Her attention was diverted to several of the stranger's quietly talking amongst themselves, their choppy dialect unfamiliar to her. Their leader, however, spoke in learned tones.

"Well?"

"I have one room available upstairs, the bunks in the barn will accommodate your men. How long were you planning on staying?"

"Maybe a month. How much?"

Warren pursed her lips. "Five silver per man per week for food and beds. Baths will be extra."

"I'll give you three silver per man per week."

"This is *my* establishment and you will pay me the amount that *I* determine."

"Then we will be off," countered Suh.

The necromancer nodded to his men, who joined Suh as he headed for the door. He was offering Warren a handsome sum, one that the owner would be hard pressed to discount.

"Four silver," shouted Warren.

"Three," responded the necromancer.

Warren chewed the inside of her cheek. Perhaps she could make up the difference some other way. "Done."

Suh turned around and approached Warren, the furtive look in the woman's eyes eliciting an inward smile. The necromancer followed Warren to a corner table and counted out the coins.

"I'll pay you on a weekly basis," he stated while handing her the owed amount.

"That's acceptable," replied Warren, weighing the leather bag full of coins in the palm of her hand.

"I want a room with a private access."

"That'll cost you extra."

"You'll be handsomely rewarded if my terms are met."

Suh and Warren locked gazes. The proprietor reached behind the bar, pulled out a key, and handed it to Suh.

"Room eleven should satisfy all of your needs. Will there be anything else? *Companionship*, perhaps?" she asked in sly tones.

Suh glared at Warren then jerked his head toward one of the brigands who followed the necromancer upstairs with his satchels.

Warren called over one of her men. "Find out who he is and why he's here."

The man walked past a slight boy with a mop of hair covering most of his eyes and a tall man with a goatee as he headed out the door. They sat at the end of the bar.

"Evening Dirk…Ben," greeted Warren, pouring them mugs of ale.

"Quite a crowd here tonight," stated Tong.

"New arrivals."

"More coins in your pocket, eh, Warren?"

"Someone has to take their money," she jested, glancing at Ben. The boy intrigued her. He never spoke nor looked up at anyone. "Hungry?"

Tong nodded and watched Warren head toward the kitchen. He leaned close to Jules' ear. "He's here. We'll sneak up the back stairs at midnight."

Jules sipped her ale while staring at her reflection. Her hair stuck out at odd angles from beneath the droopy cap; patches of dirt looked like bruises in the semi-darkness. Her breasts ached from the binding and her scalp itched from the woolen cap. Her body craved attention. Tong's nighttime trysts were tedious at best. She needed a man who could satisfy her desires. Only one man was capable of that. Wil. Jules realized too late that her strategy to kill him and then take over Graveyard was a mistake. She had had other options. Jules thought back to the countless nights she and Wil satisfied each other. There were no boundaries between them. No, that was wrong. Once their appetites were appeased, they retreated to their sides of the bed and fell asleep. They never curled up in each other's arms or shared in whispered conversation. They stimulated their minds during the day and their bodies at night. Jules frowned as the memory of Wil and the Elven woman surfaced in her mind. *Wil never offered me flowers. Or held my hand. Or invited me out to dinner.*

Jules' reflection wavered and was replaced with the elf's face. His rejection remained lodged in her mind like an itch she could not scratch. Why did he refuse her advances? Because of the woman with the red-gold hair? Ramira could never match her talents. No woman could. Jules stared into the mirror until her own face glared back at her.

~

Tong and Jules snuck up the back stairway to Suh's room, never noticing the eyes watching them from small knotholes in the wall. The brigand standing guard outside the room opened the door for them. The necromancer inserted several sheets of paper into a large leather-bound book, then turned his full attention on Tong and Jules. He pushed his unkempt hair from his forehead with dirty fingers.

"Any new information since we last met?" asked Suh.

"None."

Suh unrolled a map of the city and the surrounding area.

"We'll use the southern entrance, even though it will be the most heavily guarded. Bloodguard's capture will be easier than the elf's, so we'll focus on him first. According to Jules, he usually takes one of three streets: one to the tavern, another to the elf's house, and the third to the castle. The alleyway to the tavern is the least lit with plenty of alcoves in which to hide."

"Where do you want us to bring him?" asked Jules.

"Tie him up, gag him, and bring him here," instructed Suh.

"Bloodguard's face is well known, even here," cautioned Jules.

"No one will see him, Captain Jules, because he'll be hidden beneath a false bottom in a wagon."

Suh handed Jules two vials containing a glittering orange content. "Shake the ampoule, uncork it, and then point it at his face."

"What will happen?"

"It will dull his senses long enough for you to transport him here, Tong. Everything you do must be inconspicuous, understand?"

"You don't actually trust the thieves in this place, do you, Suh?" asked Tong.

"Of course not," replied the necromancer.

"This is the plan…keep to it, understood? Now, get out. Not you, Jules."

The brigands filed out leaving Suh and Jules alone. He offered her a glass of wine.

"Who was aboard the *Gray Wolf* when you escaped Graveyard?"

"The elf, dwarf, Abby, Ramira, and Allad." Did he suspect or know about the incident on the dock when the *Gray Wolf* landed?

"Tell me about the passengers you brought back from Caldon Island." He took a sip of wine and added, "Specifically the relationship between the woman and the elf prince."

"Ramira is Danyl's mate. They have two children. The dwarf is a king and Allad is the leader of the Herkahs."

The necromancer nodded. "Tong said that Bloodguard spends a lot of time with them."

"He does, Suh."

"Did the elf or dwarf ever meet Bloodguard on Caldon Island?"

"I don't think so, why?" Jules sensed that the necromancer was digging around for specific answers. What did he suspect?

So, thought Suh, *only Allad and this Ramira encountered Bloodguard. Is that who he wanted to place under a spell? She was the elf's mate...an unwilling partner. Did the elf know? And if he did, it was unlikely that he would befriend a man who had a tryst with his woman. Unless there was some sort of common cause...or coercion. It was time for a stroll in the city.*

"Suh?"

"That's all, Captain."

Jules exited the tavern. Did Suh know about incident after the group debarked the *Gray Wolf*? There were witnesses to the event and something as bizarre as that would certainly spread throughout Widows Point. Either the necromancer kept this knowledge to himself or he didn't know about it. Jules spotted Tong near the stables.

"What did he want, Jules?"

"He asked about the passengers on the *Gray Wolf* after we escaped from Caldon Island."

"So he didn't add any more instructions."

"No."

Tong studied her impassive features for a moment before mounting his horse. "Let's go."

~

Suh poured himself a glass of wine and mulled over the most dangerous part of his plan regarding the elf: what if he wielded the magic against him? He opened the leather-bound book and read his notes again. The potion would keep the elf in a semi-conscious state for a few hours at most. It would need to be administered every so often to keep the elf in check. With any luck, Suh's search for Demon's Breath would be brief.

Suh decided to visit the city. Using some ashes from the fireplace, he drew frown lines and furrows on his forehead. He sprinkled some cinders into his hair until it took on a dirty gray cast. He rummaged through his satchel and pulled out a heavily mended cloak. The necromancer stared at his reflection and nodded. Grabbing a crooked walking stick, he headed for Bystyn.

The ride to Bystyn lasted less than fifteen minutes. Suh noted the black tents to the left of the city and watched their even darker occupants detach themselves from the growing shadows. The necromancer blended in with groups of people entering Bystyn, including the dwarves and Herkahs. He pretended to hobble along the sidewalk, his keen eyes casually scanning the crowd. He continued on and rested against a short wall near the intersection on the eastern side. Suh did not have long to wait as the elf, his family, and Bloodguard walked over to a house fronting the square and sat on the steps.

~

Zordana spotted the necromancer, his pathetic attempt to disguise himself not fooling her. She circled around and watched him observe the individuals on the steps. *I should have known you'd sniff out the Elven magic…did you also sense the other two powers?* The wraith focused her gaze on Wil; her mind returned to the day she first saw him…

Zordana picked her way over the rock-strewn path. The sun sparkled off the bay to her left; the collection of small, wooden houses bearing blue slate tiles was clustered together on her right. The wraith angled up the trail and stopped in front of a one room house at the end of the row. Herbs were planted alongside the flat stone steps; flowerpots bursting with bright yellow and red blossoms lined the stairs. Tomatoes and other vegetables ripened beneath the sun in a garden next to the house. Chickens clucked in an enclosed pen near the garden. Zordana scowled at the permanency that these things represented. She took a deep breath and knocked on the rough-hewn door. A beautiful young woman with long brown hair opened it.

"Welcome, Zordana."

The woman stepped aside and invited Zordana to sit at the small round table. She placed a plate of food and a cup of water in front of her guest then checked on her newborn sleeping on the narrow cot.

"You have chosen to retain your appearance, I see," *stated Zordana in disappointed tones.*

"Yes, especially now," *she replied gazing at her son.*

"Is it worth it?"

"He is worth it, yes."

"Does it have a name?"

"His name is Wil."

"Why do you put up with these worthless mortals, Zaura?"

"Not all of them are evil, Zordana."

"I have yet to encounter one who isn't. What will you do if the necromancer finds you? You know he'll try to drain your blood, too."

"Zulant betrayed Zistak, remember?"

"I'm not excusing our sister's actions, Zaura, but I am concerned about your well-being."

"Wil and I are safe here."

Zordana lifted Zaura's chin and looked into her azure eyes flecked with white. Zaura gazed steadily back at her. Zordana could not fathom why she preferred living in a land where humans disrespected life so much. Time stood still in the Wold; serenity cocooned the wraiths there.

"The only safe place for you is the Wold, Zaura. Give it to one of the mortals to raise and come back home."

"I'm not leaving my son."

"It is proof of the mortals' violence!"

"I choose to remain here, Zordana."

"You will grow old and suffer from the same afflictions as the humans."

"I know."

Zordana sighed then walked over to the newborn. The baby looked at the wraith with hazel eyes; tufts of black hair sprouted up from his head. Zordana glared at the tiny creature, the urge to smother it and sever its ties with her sister barely kept in check.

"I want you to promise me something, Zordana," whispered Zaura.

The wraith looked at her.

"I want you to swear that if he ever needs help that you will be there for him."

Zordana snorted derisively. "For a mortal?"

"He's half-wraith, sister."

"You chose this life, Zaura." Zordana's voice seethed with anger. "If it needs help, it can beg for aid from its own kind."

"You choose to ignore the fact that Wil is your kin, too."

"What can I do or say to make you change your mind, Zaura?"

"Nothing."

Zordana glowered at the baby…

The cabin was replaced with the gray walls of Bystyn. Zordana stared at Wil. His revenge for Zaura's violent death was known to her, as was his rise to power on Caldon Island. Wil's defeat in Graveyard, subsequent imprisonment, and escape had filtered into the Wold as well. *Why did you come here?*

Zordana watched Zaura's son interact with Zulant's killer. Hatred for Ramira rose within her breast. Zordana glared at Suh who sat on a bench and nonchalantly glanced over at the same group on the steps. Loathing rippled across her features. The necromancer pulled his cloak more tightly against his chest, gripped his cane, and started toward the group on the steps.

"It's a lovely night, isn't it, Suh?"

Startled, the necromancer turned around and looked into the wraith's dark eyes. "Abby?"

"Call me what you wish."

The wraith's bird-like appearance was similar to Abby's, but the underlying current emanating off her was far more sinister than Zulant's was. How fortuitous in his time of wraith-blood need.

"Have we met before?"

"Yes."

"Perhaps in Widows Point?"

"Perhaps. What brings you to Bystyn, Suh?"

There was something vaguely familiar about her, something that triggered caution.

"Business."

"What draws you to those mortals?" she probed.

"Business."

"What kind of 'business', Suh?"

An eerie sensation started to encase the necromancer. An invisible net of sizzling energy spiraled its way up from his feet. Sweat beaded up on his skin and trickled down his face leaving garish streaks of gray in their wake. Suh smudged the damp residue with his hand. She was unmasking him without lifting a finger. The power this wraith exuded left him feeling anxious and energized at the same time. He glanced at the group on the stoop then back to the wraith. She was gone.

Zordana watched him search for her from within the shadows of a garden near Sophie's home. The condescending smile on her face faded when a low growling filled her ears. Blue crouched within the darkness, her emerald eyes ablaze. A pair of yellow eyes appeared in the branches above the cat's head. Blue's attention shifted upward then back to the wraith. Zordana flinched when Blue bared her teeth and hissed.

"What sort of creature are you that can identify a wraith?"

Blue inched closer to the wraith; her ears lay flat against her head. Zordana recoiled when the big cat's formidable claws dug into the ground. The wraith slowly retreated, fearing that the creature would launch itself at her.

"Come, Ceela; our work here is done…at least for tonight."

Blue started as a rush of air stirred her fur. She snarled once then padded over to the stoop. Kayla and Wyl slept peacefully together in a woven basket. A soft, woolen blanket covered the children. The cat climbed inside with her charges. Her half-lidded eyes and flicking tail warned against anyone who wished to do them harm.

Hanna wiped her hands on her apron then untied it and hung it on the hook behind the door. She blew out the lamps, grabbed a bottle of wine from the rack, and then headed up to her rooms. She had plenty of time to freshen up before Wil called on her. Hanna unlocked the door and was about to walk in when someone grabbed her from behind. She was bound and gagged within seconds. Pushed onto the couch, Hanna looked up at a young boy, a tall man with a goatee, and three other men standing by the door. The boy, she quickly realized, was the one who tried to caution her about Wil. He sat down beside her.

"You didn't take my warning seriously, did you?"

The silky voice, Hanna realized, belonged to a woman.

"My name is Jules, and you're going to help us abduct Wil."

Hanna shook her head. Jules slapped her hard across the face in response.

"I'm not *asking* you…I'm *telling* you!" Jules sneered at Hanna, the desire to cut her throat controlled only by needing the woman to get to Wil. Besides, it would be so much more satisfying to slay her in front of him.

"There are so many beautiful women in this city and, yet, he chose *you*? What does he see in you?"

Hanna kept her expression stoic.

"Wil and I spent many, *many* nights in bed together." Jules' voice oozed with spite. "There wasn't one inch of our bodies that we didn't explore."

Hanna did not react, which angered Jules.

"His talents will be wasted on such a mundane woman as yourself. He…."

"I hate to interrupt, Jules, but we have to reassess our plan," grumbled Tong. "Suh wanted us to move Wil under the cover of darkness."

"So we're a few hours ahead of schedule."

"Your arrogance is going to cost all of us," he reproached her.

Contempt filled Jules' face as she snatched the bag from Tong. She carefully unrolled the glass bottles filled with an orange powder and handed one to Tong and the other to one of the men. Jules motioned for two of the men to keep watch in the alley across from the building.

"Make sure you cover your nose and mouth when you break this at Bloodguard's feet," she reminded the brigand as he left the room.

Jules sat next to Hanna and pulled out a knife. "I'll slice your throat if you warn him, understood?"

Hanna nodded; Jules removed the gag.

"Why are you doing this?"

"Because he belongs to *me*," she hissed.

Tong subtly shook his head while testing the edge of his knife with his thumb. Jules' plans for Bloodguard would resume once Suh was finished with him. That is, if Bloodguard were still alive. Tong doubted that the pirate would jump back into bed with her regardless of her skills. He studied Jules' features, which fluctuated between jealousy and vengeance. Her personal plans were going to clash with the necromancer's schemes, and that would not end well for any of them. Tong glanced at the bound woman, who remained calm despite the circumstances.

Hanna focused her attention on her predicament. Jules' resentment toward her was disturbing at best. She had no idea what, if anything, happened between Jules and Wil. Jules revealed enough about him to corroborate some of what he mentioned during their dinner the other night. *He's a pirate and a murderer. He used to raid and pillage a lot of the ports on Caldon Island,* resonated in her mind. Wil's voice drifted into her head. *I was a businessman on Caldon Island.* Hanna squeezed her eyes shut and tried to force the conflicting yet somehow similar words out of her thoughts. She had to remain composed and think clearly. Hanna did not want to aggravate the volatile woman nor jeopardize Wil's life. Or her own.

Jules paced back and forth then walked to the windows and peered out onto the street below. The minutes turned into an hour and still no Bloodguard. Two hours later they heard someone climbing the stairs. Hanna tensed up while Tong repositioned himself by the door. Jules yanked Hanna to her feet and forced her to the door. The captain's knife remained poised across her neck.

"Hanna?" Wil called out while knocking on the door.

Jules pulled Hanna's hair back, exposing more of her throat.

"Just a moment!"

Wil heard a scraping sound behind him and turned just as the brigand smashed the vial at his feet. The pirate shielded his face; Wil instinctively brought his arms up to ward off the swirling mist but was too slow. Bloodguard collapsed against the door and into unconsciousness.

Tong opened the door and let Bloodguard fall into the room. He and the other pirate dragged him in and closed the door. They bound Wil's hands and feet then left him on the floor. Jules knelt down beside him and turned his head toward her. A disquieting look crossed her features.

Panic lodged in Hanna's mind while she watched them tie Wil up. "What are you going to do with him?"

"The wagon is in the alleyway, Jules," said Tong, ignoring Hanna. "What do you want to do with her?"

"Bring her along."

"She's not part of Suh's plan."

"I'm not giving her to Suh," she responded.

"What are you going to do with Wil?"

Jules strode toward Hanna then brought her fist down on her head. The elf crumpled to the floor. Jules fished through Wil's pockets and pulled out his key.

"Wait for me," she ordered.

Jules kept to the gloomy alleyways on her way to Bloodguard's room. Opening the door, she lit a lamp and began to search for any valuables. A single chest of drawers stood against the far wall. Two drawers held his neatly folded clothing; the other two were empty. She handled every item and, finding nothing of value, discarded them on the floor. Jules rummaged through his night stand. It contained a few toiletries.

"Where did you stash your valuables, *my love*?"

Jules crossed her arms and scanned the room. The chest, night stand, bed, a small table, and a couple of chairs were all it contained. She chewed on her lower lip in thought then nodded her head. She lay on the floor in front of the dresser and ran her fingers along its underside. Disappointed but not deterred, she repeated her action on the night stand. Nothing. On a whim, she pulled the drawer all the way out and flipped it over. Wil's leather pouch was stuffed into a makeshift frame. Jules pried it loose.

"Let's see what you have."

She untied the leather cord and dumped the contents on his bed. After a quick count, she realized there was enough money and gem stones to live very comfortably for quite some time. Jules checked the other drawers and found one other bag. She undid the tie and deposited a small glass vial filled with silver liquid next to the other pile. Picking it up, she shook the ampoule. Jules uncorked it and sniffed the contents. She detected a slight metallic odor.

"You would only hide something of value, *my love*," she muttered recorking the phial.

Satisfied that she had retrieved anything of value, Jules left to rejoin Tong and the others.

While Jules ransacked Wil's room, Tong and the pirates rolled the unmoving pair into blankets then hoisted them over their shoulders.

The limp bodies were placed in the fake bottom of the cart and then hidden from view with wooden planks. Tong kept an eye out for Jules while pretending to adjust the straps and halters on the horses. The added risk the elf woman presented concerned him. What would happen if her family or friends decided to look for her? Alerting the elves to her disappearance before the rest of the plan was set in motion could place them all in jeopardy. And for what? Jules' ridiculous obsession with Bloodguard?

The long shadows stretched past the lane he waited in and provided concealment for Jules, who joined Tong fifteen minutes later. Seated on the wagon, Tong slapped the reins down on the horses' back.

"Where are the others?" she asked while adjusting her cap.

"On their way to the inn," replied Tong, guiding the horse down the main avenue.

Jules rearranged her bangs to cover more of her face as they neared the main gate. Tong nodded to the guards before the wide tunnel swallowed them up; they emerged onto the plains moments later.

"How long will Bloodguard be out?" he asked.

"At least an hour or so, according to Suh."

"Where are you going to keep the woman?"

"With Wil."

"Suh may not agree."

"Wil's cooperation will increase if he senses she's in danger, Tong."

"Continuing to veer from the plan will only *increase* the risks against us, Jules."

"I'll take full responsibility for her."

Yes, you will, he thought.

They maneuvered around the Dragon's Backbone and pulled around to the stairs at the back of the inn. They ignored Warren's men sitting on the porch and near the stables once they rode around the giant rocks. One of the men disappeared inside the tavern. Tong and the men unloaded their cargo and carried them up the back stairway into Suh's rooms. Curious, the necromancer picked up the corners of the blankets covering their heads.

"Who's she?" he demanded in an irritated voice.

"His love interest," replied Jules pointing her chin at Bloodguard.

"Get rid of her."

"Not so fast, Suh," Jules said. "She'll be useful to us."

"In what way?"

"Bloodguard might be more obliging."

Suh processed the information. The captain made a good point.

"Use her *then* kill her," added Jules.

Moaning broke into their conversation. Both Wil and Hanna were returning to consciousness. The pirates tied Wil in a chair; they dragged Hanna to the corner of the room.

Wil's head pounded; his lungs hurt. He opened his eyes and steeled himself until the room ceased spinning. Shadows formed into men; voices became recognizable. Wil tried to focus on the closest man.

"Captain Wil Bloodguard!"

Suh. Wil cringed inwardly.

"Your survival abilities are remarkable."

"Well met, *my love*," Jules whispered seductively in his ear.

Wil squeezed his eyes shut then reopened them. His vision returned. Bloodguard stared from one face to the other then sucked in his breath when he spotted a bruised Hanna in the corner. He watched her work herself into a sitting position, her gaze never leaving him.

Suh wrote a letter, sealed it, and then handed it to one of his men. The pirate nodded and left.

"I should have killed you in Graveyard," began Suh, "or been more thorough in the woods outside the city. Speaking of that," the necromancer pressed, leaning close to Wil, "who were you *entertaining* in the forest, Captain?"

Wil glared at the necromancer.

"Was it her?" Suh pointed at Hanna. "No...she seems like a willing partner. Who did you place under a spell, Bloodguard?"

"Piss off, Suh."

Hanna noticed Wil's anger simmering just below the surface. Wil didn't deny Suh's accusation. Was the necromancer right?

One of the men bumped into the table holding the box of Gaulthea vine branches, which fell to the floor and exposed the contents.

"Clumsy fool!" growled Suh.

He turned back to Bloodguard who wrinkled his nose in distaste. The necromancer stared at him for a moment then checked the expressions on everyone else in the room. He detected mainly boredom.

"Everyone get out," he ordered.

Forgotten in the corner, Hanna watched and listened.

Suh picked up the box and held it close to Wil, who grimaced in response. Only a wraith could detect the vines' scent. He rubbed it across Wil's skin- Bloodguard fidgeted in his seat.

"What are you doing?" asked Wil. "What is that?"

Half wraith? What's the other half? Man? Certainly not elf. Half wraith. Half wraith. I don't remember seeing any male wraiths in the Wold...only females. Your father was a man. The only wraiths that left the Wold with me were Zistak, Zulant, and Zaura, who ran away....

Wil noted the concentration on Suh's face; the necromancer hadn't blinked in a long time. An uneasy feeling grew within him while watching the necromancer struggle with some sort of enigma. He glanced over at Hanna, who continued to look at him from across the room. Her face was unreadable.

We'll get out of this, Wil mouthed to her.

She flinched when Suh abruptly focused his attention on Wil.

"Your mother...who was she?"

"None of your business."

The necromancer struck Wil across the face. Hanna started at the sudden assault.

"Answer my question!"

Wil turned his head away from him. Suh walked over and hauled Hanna to her feet. He forced her to kneel in front of Wil and placed the edge of his knife against her throat.

"I won't ask again."

"Evie…her name was Evie!"

"All wraith names begin with the letter 'Z'."

Confusion rippled across Wil's face. "What makes you think my mother was a wraith?"

The necromancer shoved the Gaulthea vine into Wil's face then nodded when the pirate tried to jerk his head away. Other than being annoyed by his action, Hanna did not react to the plant.

"Only a wraith can smell this."

Wil stared off into the distance.

"Her name was Zaura, wasn't it?"

Wil looked into Hanna's eyes and saw fear and uncertainty within them. He had to find some way to keep her alive.

"Her name was Evie."

Suh pushed Hanna aside then searched through his bag. He produced a needle. Grabbing a handful of hair, Suh forced Wil's head to one side and jammed it into his jugular vein. Wil sucked in air through clenched teeth; Hanna turned away from the necromancer's barbarity. Suh removed the needle and watched the blood dribble into a small vial.

Suh swished the contents. The blood was red. The necromancer combined the ingredients to make a simple flame then added a few drops of Wil's blood. Nothing happened. He altered the mixtures with the same results. The blood was too diluted with mortal blood. The necromancer doubled and then tripled the amount of Wil's blood to no avail. Suh glared at Wil.

Wil started to laugh. "I guess I'm human after all."

Suh pulled up a chair and sat across from Bloodguard to pursue another vexing mystery. "Who did you give the aphrodisiac to?"

"I accidentally broke the bottle and suffered the potion's effects on my own."

Suh's voice was laced with disdain. "You must have been very *frustrated*."

"The worst three hours of my life."

"Where's Abby?"

The question caught Wil by surprise. "I heard she headed west with the Herkahs."

"That's what I heard, too," agreed the necromancer. "Who did you sleep with in the forest, Captain Bloodguard?"

"No one."

"You're a liar. Where's Abby, Bloodguard?"

"I don't know."

"Again a lie. You know that Abby is a wraith, don't you?"

"Yes."

"And how do you know this?"

"I heard that rumor on Caldon Island," lied Wil.

"Who did you sleep with in the forest?"

"Myself."

A knock on the door suspended the interrogation. Tong peered in and jerked his head at Suh, who left the room.

Hanna gazed at Wil. The man seemed to sag in the chair; his chin rested on his chest. Blood ceased trickling from the puncture wound in his neck.

"How are you feeling?" she asked in a hushed voice.

His head ached and the bruise on his cheek felt hot. The nausea would not go away. "Terrific."

"Suh really believes that your mother was a wraith…is that why he siphoned some of your blood?"

"He mixes wraith blood with his potions…it's how he fabricates his magic," he explained.

"But your mother…."

"My mother was not a wraith."

Hanna studied the man who would not look at her. Uncertainty and a faltering sense of who he was replaced his usual self-assuredness. She saw him struggle with his inner turmoil and the helplessness of their current situation.

Wil's mind churned. How did he know her name? She couldn't have been a wraith. She was beautiful and kind…a loving mother who

81

never hurt anyone.

"They're going to kill us, aren't they?" she asked after a while.

"Eventually."

"Good to know," she replied in sardonic tones.

Jules sauntered back into the room and sat on Wil's lap facing him. An evil smile played on her lips while he glared with contempt at her. She stroked his hair then glanced over at Hanna, who subtly shook her head in disgust.

"I should have ended your worthless life in Graveyard, whore," Wil declared.

Jules smiled seductively and kissed him on the forehead. He tried to jerk his head away but she held it fast.

"I'll throttle you if given half a chance."

"You won't get that chance, Wil," she purred, then stood up.

"Yes, I will," he growled.

Jules walked over to Hanna and placed her hands on her hips. The bound woman appeared nervous but unafraid. Jules crouched down and grabbed Hanna by the throat.

"Leave her be, Jules," warned Wil. "She has nothing to do with any of this."

"What are you going to do to stop me?"

Hatred filled Wil's eyes.

"I thought so," she sniffed, then turned her attention back to Hanna. "Did Wil ever tell you about the *Wild Dog Tavern* incident? No? Well, let me enlighten you about your love interest's *true* character."

"Stop it, Jules."

"Caldon Island's coastline is dotted with villages, ports, and any number of small towns. Most are nothing more than collections of homesteads manned by fishermen and their families. Midway between Graveyard and Port Quint was a settlement known for trading precious jewels from the northern section of the island. The *Wild Dog Tavern* was where all the transactions took place."

"Don't listen to her, Hanna."

"I had been under Wil's tutelage for about six months when he decided to invade the settlement and claim the gem trade for his own. Hundreds of his men descended upon the town while several vessels sailed into the harbor. It didn't take long to subdue everyone, but that wasn't enough for you, was it, *my love*?"

Loathing for Jules filled Wil's face, which elicited satisfaction on Jules' visage.

"Wil entered the *Wild Dog Tavern* and demanded exclusive rights to all commodities traded in the settlement. The master of the town reminded Wil that they were under Suh's protection and that he would demand retribution for Wil's unprecedented attack. Do you know what Wil did? He decapitated the master and ordered his men to slaughter anyone who stood against him."

Hanna turned to Wil. "Is this true?"

"Yes…but she left out a few crucial details."

"What did I leave out?"

"That Suh orchestrated the ruse to get me there and then ambushed me and my men."

"Your greed and keen desire to expand your territory compelled you to attack, *my love*."

He looked at Hanna who stared at him with disbelief. Jules' wicked chuckling drew his attention back to her. His agitation increased her satisfaction as much as the look of disbelief on Hanna's face.

"Ask him when he comes back in."

"He's commencing with his plan," stated Jules.

Apprehension wormed its way through his mind. "And that is?"

"He's inviting another guest to join us," explained Jules while sliding her hands seductively up Wil's thighs.

"Who?"

"Your dear friend Danyl."

The hunger in her eyes turned his stomach. Fear for the elf's safety rose to the forefront regardless of Danyl's ability to wield his magic. Wil's mouth opened when he realized that Suh's plan was to take the

Green Might.

"You're suddenly quite pale, *my love*."

"You're using us as bait?"

"Please…don't flatter yourself," said Jules.

The door opened; Tong nodded for Jules. She smiled at them then left.

"She's quite the prize," muttered Hanna.

"She was a mistake," he replied in cold tones.

"How long did you entertain this 'mistake'?"

"For too long."

Wil shifted in his chair to alleviate the bonds digging into his wrists and ankles but he could do nothing to ease the tightness in his chest. He wanted to explain everything to Hanna but that, he was sure, would make things worse.

"You must hate me," he said in a quiet voice. "I can't blame you if you do."

"How many more people will you kill before you're satisfied?" she asked after a long silence.

"Just two more."

SIX

The two remaining Kreetch forged ahead, their week-long trek through the mountains filled with twists, turns, and doubling back to find a way out. The sluggish river blocking their way forward provided the greatest challenge for them. The demons zigzagged over unstable rock crossings until the river narrowed several miles to the east. A wide ledge spanned the waterway where all of the Brethren could traverse. The pair scrabbled over boulders and squeezed between several crevasses where they found themselves in a vast cavity. The stuffy odors of the confined spaces were replaced with a hint of fresh air. The demons followed the scent and, less than an hour later, spotted a pinpoint of light up ahead. Relieved, the demons scrambled toward the light and out from under the oppressive weight of the mountain.

They blinked at the late afternoon sun that shone down on the corridor. Boulders and clusters of pines marked the boundary between the range and the forest. The demons ambled toward the woods in search of food. Animals and birds scurried or flew out of their tired grasps. They moved deeper into the forest where the shadows hid them from their prey. The demons squatted behind a fallen tree and waited for something – anything - to come within easy reach. They spotted a buck about twenty yards to their right and were about to give chase when two huntsmen came into view to their left.

The elves silently raised their bows and concentrated their arrows on the animal. They took aim then watched the buck sprint away from them. Birds suddenly took flight as two distorted shapes lunged at the hunters, who fumbled for their knives. They were too slow. The demons tore into the elves, whose screams echoed into silence. Sated, the demons entered the mountain and headed back to their kin.

~

Ignoring Wil, Hanna, and Jules, Suh paced across the room with his hands clasped in the small of his back. There was no doubt that Wil was half wraith, yet the man's blood provided no power for his potions. Did his human half dilute the wraith blood? The necromancer pulled up a chair and sat in front of Wil, his dark eyes focused on the brigand.

"Who was your father?"

"I don't know."

"When was the last time you saw Abby?"

"When you attacked Graveyard."

"Who did you sleep with in the forest, Bloodguard?"

"Myself."

Jules stood and stretched. She stuffed her hands in her pockets and wrapped her fingers around the vial. She had forgotten about it until now. "I found this in his room," she said, handing it to the necromancer.

An evil smile crossed Suh's face as he held up the full vial of wraith blood.

A cold sensation settled into Wil's bones while watching the wicked elation on Suh's face.

"Wraith blood," whispered the necromancer. "Jules…you and Tong prepare for the next phase of my plan.

~

A commotion within the vast chamber caught Sul-Tak's attention. Moments later two Kreetch approached him.

"Did you find a way out?"

The lower demons jumped up and down while motioning in the direction they had just come from.

"How long will it take us?"

The Kreetch exchanged confused looks. Sul-Tak disregarded them then counted the days they had been gone. He estimated that it would take several days. The Brethren were well rested and full - they would leave now. He motioned for the Kreetch to lead them.

Travel was slow for the Brethren, who scrambled over narrow outcroppings and inched their way through tight gaps in a single file. The Kreetch led them deeper into the mountain. Sul-Tak's doubt that they'd ever see daylight again was lessened by the demons' unflagging push forward. He lost count of the days then concentrated on not falling into a chasm or getting stuck in one of the narrow breaches in the rock. The mountain took its share of skin and blood as they continued on.

The Kreetch guided the demons to the narrowest part of the river. The luminescent veins spreading along the surface of the vast cavern reflected off the impenetrable black water. The Kreetch were about to cross over when something caught Sul-Tak's attention. He noticed light reflecting off a branch lodged against some rocks a few yards away. Curious, he maneuvered toward it and glanced down at the object.

"The Ankh-Nam!"

He lay on his stomach and reached for the branch. Pulling it to him, he reverently lifted the amulet up for all the Brethren to see. Whispered snarling and whining filled the rocky chamber. Sul-Tak placed it in his pocket and smiled, for the priceless talisman was now safely back in the Brethren's possession.

Reinvigorated with the Ankh-Nam, the demons continued their arduous trek. The Brethren, like the two Kreetch, noticed the change in the air. They surged toward the bright point of light and back out onto the land.

~

A shadow kept to the darkness as it made its way along the side streets to the house off the main avenue. It silently looked around, opened the gate, and walked up to the front door. It slid a piece of paper under it and left as soundlessly as it arrived.

~

"How much time will you need?" asked Danyl the next morning.

"Two…maybe three hours should be enough to get everything in order."

She kissed Wyl and then handed him to Sophie. Danyl gathered Kayla in his arms.

"Are you sure you don't need my help?"

"No, Sophie; thank you anyway."

Danyl peered outside. Dark clouds threatened rain. "We should go before we get drenched."

Ramira watched them leave. Danyl and Sophie headed to the castle. Ramira smiled and then set about her chores. She straightened up the bedrooms and then headed downstairs. A piece of paper near the front door caught her attention. Picking it up, she broke the seal and read it.

I have Bloodguard and the elf woman. If you want to see them alive again, then meet me at the tavern a short ride south of the city. Come alone or they die.

"What sort of prank is this?" she muttered out loud then dropped the note on the kitchen table.

Ramira grabbed her cloak, strapped on her knives, and headed for Wil's room. She cautiously climbed the stairs and walked over to the door. It was ajar. Ramira slid her blades out and pushed the door open. The room was littered with overturned drawers and piles of clothing. She scrutinized everything. Someone was very thorough in their search…but for what?

Ramira headed for the tavern in the steady rain. The annoyed proprietor mumbled under his breath while grabbing the linens from the tables. She sneaked past the busy innkeeper and up the staircase. Ramira checked the landing for anyone loitering in the short hallway. Satisfied, she approached the door and pushed down on the handle.

Warily entering the room, she peered inside. Ramira fingered the dried smudges on the door. Several glasses stood on the counter; the blanket on the sofa was bunched up. Ramira entered the bedroom. Hanna's bed was made.

I have Bloodguard and the elf woman. If you want to see them alive again, then meet me at the tavern an hour south of the city. Come alone or they die.

"Who would abduct them and why?"

Ramira thought of their current situation. Other than the dwarves' encounter with the lone Kreetch, nothing seemed out of the ordinary. This, however, reeked of a trap. Was the letter meant for her or Danyl? If Danyl was supposed to have found it…*Suh*. The necromancer was back and wanted the Elven magic. He knew that the only reason Danyl would come was to save Wil and Hanna.

"You're going to regret this," she hissed.

Ramira kept beneath the eaves while making her way to the stables. She called for a horse then sped out of Bystyn beneath a driving rain and approached the tavern less than twenty minutes later. She steered her mount around the Dragon's Backbone and dismounted. Ramira tied the reins to the rails and walked past the men on the porch and into the tavern. The rain abruptly ceased. Ramira stood just inside the doorway and studied the men while water dripped off her cloak and pooled around her boots. She shoved the hood off her head.

"You honor my humble establishment with your presence, Lady Ramira!" Warren's mocking tone drew laughter from her patrons.

"Where are they?" she demanded.

Warren placed her hands on the bar top and smiled craftily at her. "I don't know what you're talking about, Lady Ramira."

"I'll not ask again," she warned.

She sensed movement behind her. "I will kill anyone foolish enough to assail me."

Chairs scraped across the wooden floor; Warren subtly nodded to the men approaching Ramira from behind.

In one swift movement, Ramira flung her cloak over the nearest man then brought her knives across the throats of two others. Three more men lunged forward and met the same fate. She caught someone running up the stairs from the corner of her eye.

~

Zordana watched the commotion from the concealing hedging near the Dragon's Backbone. She narrowed her eyes at the woman efficiently slaying the men that lunged toward her through the inn's large windows. The wraith's ire rose from the deepest recesses of her soul while she glared at the mortal who slew her sister. Zordana would not fail like Zulant had.

Suh glanced sourly at the unseen disturbance while combining the ingredients for the Unspeakable. The door opened; a nervous pirate walked in.

"What's going on downstairs?"

"She's here, Suh," he replied, wringing his hands.

"Who's here?" Suh turned his full attention on the man.

"The woman with the red-gold hair. She's downstairs. She just killed six men."

Ramira! What in blazes is she doing here? Wil looked at Hanna, who sat up against the wall.

"She picked up the letter instead of the elf," murmured Suh, who then smiled. "He'll come for sure now."

Footsteps marked the progression of someone climbing the steps; bodies toppling to the floor indicated who that was. The door opened; the pirate who brought the news backed away from Ramira.

Wil noted the murderous rage on her face; Hanna pushed herself against the wall.

The necromancer absently swirled the contents of the phial while studying the dangerous woman standing a few feet away. He had never seen her close-up before. Her amethyst eyes glittered dangerously; her flawless skin glowed in the lamplight. His gaze traveled to her knives, which continued to drip blood on the floor. It was too bad that he hadn't prepared one of his sleeping potions.

"I'll take them now, Suh."

Ramira walked past the necromancer and cut their bonds. Wil helped Hanna to her feet; she clung to his arm.

Suh cocked his head and slowly pulled the wraith blood out of his pocket. He uncorked the bottle with his teeth then poised it over the other vial. Ramira glared at him.

"I think not."

Ramira took a step toward him; Suh angled the ampoules closer together.

"A stalemate, Suh?"

Armed men entered the room, stood outside the door, and shuffled up the staircase. Ramira remained still while imperceptibly urging Wil and Hanna closer to her.

"You cannot possibly best all of these men with your knives, can you?" Suh's oily voice grated on her nerves.

"I only have to slay one man, Suh."

"My plans are already in progress, Ramira. If you wait long enough you will be reunited with your mate and children."

"Liar."

"Did you happen to see Captain Jules and Tong anywhere? No? They are in Bystyn completing the best part of my scheme."

Hatred seethed on Ramira's face.

"If I'm not mistaken, your mate and a woman took your children to the castle on the corner this morning, did they not?"

"He's baiting you, Ramira," cautioned Wil.

"I am going to rip you apart with my bare hands if you lay one finger on my family," she breathed hard at Suh.

Suh was about to reply when he noticed the potion's yellowish hue begin to fluctuate. He corked the wraith blood vial and stowed it in his pocket, his gaze fixed on the Unspeakable that began to boil then steam in his hand. Time seemed to stand still as the liquid transformed into glittering black. Shocked, he looked at Ramira: she was a demon.

The sparkling blackness shot out of the bottle and swirled up to the ceiling. It looked like a piece of the night sky. The men scrambled out of the room and tavern.

An ominous sensation grabbed hold of Ramira while she watched the potion change. She instinctively grasped Wil's and Hanna's hands and pulled them to the floor when the haze escaped the bottle. The Source of Darkness roiled within her soul and sprang to life. The magic enveloped the trio when a resounding boom and a searing wind obliterated the tavern. Ramira felt something latch onto her leg. Suh. A white-hot explosion followed a second later.

Hidden behind the largest boulders of the Dragon's Backbone, Zordana observed them through the window as Zulant's murderess entered the room. The necromancer held up a vial and poised another vessel near its edge. Wil and the woman edged to the murderess's side while the necromancer gestured toward them. She adjusted the strap on her shoulder and pushed her satchel behind her. A pair of unblinking yellow eyes was visible within the shadowy boughs.

"How fortunate am I to witness your deaths," she whispered. "Go ahead, Necromancer… mix the potions."

The smirk on her face turned into a line and then a frown when the contents erupted. Uncertainty morphed into panic when a wall of sparkling amethysts surrounded them, including the necromancer. A brilliant white light pulsed once.

"This cannot be…." breathed a stunned Zordana.

A blistering hot wind tore through the glade making it difficult to breathe. The air seemed to compress around her; the crackling energy irritated her skin. The gyrating column expanded beyond the room, demolishing everything it came into contact with. Zordana dove behind the boulders and blocked her ears as the resounding explosion obliterated everything within the clearing, including her screams.

Zada smiled at Seven, who played with Kayla on the sofa. She giggled whenever the dwarf blew raspberries on her belly. The Elven king held his sleeping grandson in his arms, sheer contentment etched on his face.

"I'm still going to teach them how to shoot a bow and arrow," teased Danyl. "You'll be an easy target because of your wider backside and slower feet!"

"My keen dwarven instinct will warn me when these little imps are on the hunt," countered Seven good-naturedly while picking Kayla up.

"Is your 'keen dwarven instinct' aware of the fact that my granddaughter just peed on your tunic?"

"You're just like your Uncle Styph," chuckled Seven. He kissed Kayla and then handed her to Danyl. "I'll be right back."

Clare stifled a laugh but the others could not.

"Your children have brought great joy to this household," she said to Danyl while he changed her diaper.

"I've never been so happy, Zada. I just wish that my mother was alive to share this with us."

Back in her father's arms, Kayla searched the room for the dwarf king.

Zada's inner sight clicked on. The room disappeared and was replaced by the grainy blackness of the in-between world. Nothing moved within it. Apprehension began to build in Zada's mind as the silent corridor remained open. A blinding white light abruptly exploded followed by a brilliant amethyst glow. A thunderous boom erupted a second later. The in-between place slammed shut. Zada collapsed into Allad's arms but still felt the rolling tremors beneath her feet. She opened her eyes and stared at the items rattling on the table. She looked from one startled face to the other. The sudden cessation of sound and movement left everyone speechless. Everyone except for Kayla and Wyl, who began to cry. Danyl picked up Wyl and Clare held Kayla. Neither child responded to their attempts to soothe them.

"What in the Four Corners of the land was that?" the Elven king finally asked.

"An earthquake?" offered Seven.

"Any idea, Zada?"

The nomad shook her head no.

PART TWO

SEVEN

Wil opened his eyes and then staggered to his feet. A sense of panic gripped him while searching for Ramira and Hanna.

"Ramira? Hanna?"

Moaning caught his attention. He scrambled behind a fallen log and found both women bruised but otherwise unharmed. Wil helped them sit on the tree trunk. He noticed Hanna staring at Ramira.

"What happened?" he asked.

"That fool combined the wrong ingredients," growled Ramira.

Hanna gaped at Ramira. "You house magic?"

"Yes."

Wil, she noted, kept his gaze averted. "You knew, didn't you, Wil?"

Wil nodded.

"What else should I know?" she asked in apprehensive tones.

"Suh is here with us."

"How do you know that?" asked Wil.

"Because I felt him grab onto my leg. The magic protected him like it did the rest of us."

"We have to find him," said Wil.

"First, we need to get back to the city," stated Ramira, "and warn the others."

The trio headed north, the dense forest slowing their progress. The woods finally thinned out hours later revealing the plains. Something, however, was very wrong. The forest in the north stretched farther south than they remembered; no houses or patrols dotted the landscape. Standing on a rise, they could see a vast vertical scar along the mountains to the north and gigantic piles of gray rocks and boulders that had flattened miles of forest at their feet. Bystyn was nowhere to be seen.

"Are we too far east or west?" asked Wil.

Ramira turned around and scanned the woods to the south. The trees were too concentrated and much taller than she remembered. The plains should be miles wider. A sick feeling erupted in her stomach. *What did you do, Suh?*

Disorientated, Hanna, too, scrutinized their surroundings, which appeared familiar yet strange at the same time.

"Well? Too far east or west?" repeated Wil.

Long shadows stained the ground where Bystyn should stand. The sound of running water drew their attention to the Ahltyn, which flowed in a narrow waterway to their right. They headed for the river and drank until their thirst was quenched. A space between a pair of large slabs of rock offered protection from the elements and any predators that might lurk about during the night. They collected wood and dead leaves then deposited them into a depression. Muttering obscenities under his breath, Wil impatiently rubbed two sticks together until the dried leaves finally caught fire. The trio huddled around the flames for warmth; sleep did not come easily for any of them.

They awoke stiff and hungry the next morning. Hanna and Wil scavenged for anything edible and were grateful when Ramira brought back a rabbit. She placed it over a makeshift spit and watched the fat drip onto the flames.

Wil sat with his elbows on his knees, his gaze focused on the blade of grass he absently twirled between his fingers. Suh's accusatory words regarding his mother echoed in his mind. *All wraith names begin with the letter 'Z'. Only a wraith can smell this. Her name was Zaura, wasn't it?* How did the necromancer know his mother's name? Wil thought of his mother. She never spoke a mean word nor crumbled beneath the hard life she lived. They never went without food and, although heavily mended, their clothes were always clean. But it was the times that they spent together that he remembered most fondly. She'd read to him in the evenings and taught him about the world in which they lived. The glade wavered and was replaced with a memory of him as a young boy…

Wil sat on the front stoop and stared out across the vast ocean. Rolling swells deposited driftwood and shells upon the shoreline that was interspersed with dark gray rocks. Gulls floated on the water or rode the wind currents high in the air. A warm breeze tugged on his hair and clothing. Fishermen tied up their small boats along the rickety pier. The men placed their catch on carts and pulled them to the fish shop at the end of the wharf. Their children raced to them as they stepped onto the worn path leading to the village. The men ruffled their hair; laughter drifted up to where he sat. He wondered what it would be like to have his father at his side. His mother handed him a glass of lemonade and then joined him on the step.

"Do you want to go to Widows Point with me tomorrow?" she asked.

"Are we going to the sweet shop, Ma?"

"We can stop in, if you want."

He nodded.

"What's on your mind, Wil?"

"Where's my Pa?"

"I don't know, Wil."

"Did he go away?"

Zaura nodded.

"Will he ever come back?"

"I don't think so."

"Why not? Did you two fight?" he persisted.

"Things didn't...work out for us," she replied in a quiet voice. "He did, however, leave the best part of himself with me."

"What's that, Ma?"

She stroked his hair and wrapped her arms around him. "You."

Cold penetrated into the warmth of the late afternoon by the sea; shaking ripped him from his reverie. Wil opened his eyes and sighed.

"Where did you just go to?" asked Ramira.

Wil collected himself and tossed the blade of grass onto the ground. Suh's words continued to reverberate in his head. They clashed with what he understood and magnified the absent facts of his

99

young life. No family. No father. But he had his mother, whose calming presence and gentle encouragement kept the rest of the disappointments at bay.

Hanna knew nothing about magic or potions, only that both brought the three of them to wherever they were. Separating the fruit and nuts into three piles, the elf thought about the wielder of the Green Might. Those who brandished it usually succumbed to the power, with death being the result. Danyl was the exception. She glanced at Ramira, who tended to the spit with a far-away look in her eyes.

"Not many people know about your magic, do they, Ramira?"

"No."

"I can't imagine shouldering such a responsibility."

Ramira thought back to all the people who died solely because one demon coveted the Source of Darkness. She understood that her demon heritage and nearly being turned into the Black Queen wasn't her fault. Her solace rested in the home she shared with Danyl and her children. The normalcy offered within those walls alleviated the overwhelming duty that fate placed on both their shoulders.

They shared a frugal meal of berries, nuts, and rabbit in silence. The rising sun chased away the shadows and chilly air. The trio occasionally scrutinized their surroundings, searching for anything that looked familiar. None of them succeeded.

"We should set out for Bystyn," suggested Ramira after they finished eating.

They headed in a northeasterly direction, never noticing the shadows paralleling their course. The dense woods muffled all sounds and blocked most of their sight.

"Is the scar on your forehead compliments of Suh?" asked Hanna after a while.

"I have other mementos from him, too."

"Did he burn you in the woods?" she pursued.

Wil halted and spun around to face her. "Yes, in the woods after I spent hours pleasuring myself because the vial containing the aphrodisiac broke. Any more questions?"

"I hope that *that* was less strenuous than your fire-starting skills."

Hanna's deadpan tone forced Ramira to bite her tongue.

Wil glared at them. "You two find that funny?"

Ramira laughed so hard that she snorted; Hanna continued to chuckle. Grumbling, Wil threw his hands up in the air. He spun around to continue on without them and came face to face with an elf with emerald green eyes.

"Danyl!" Wil shouted with relief at his friend.

The elf's unrelenting gaze startled Wil.

"Why aren't you as happy to see us as we are you?" asked Wil.

The elf studied the trio, his eyes widening with recognition when he noticed Ramira.

"Because," Ramira said in faltering tones, "that's not Danyl."

~

Zordana rose from behind the protection of the Dragon's Backbone and gasped at the destruction. The inn and surrounding trees were reduced to splinters; black smoke rose upward from the gaping hole where the building once stood. Nothing within the immediate area survived. The ripple in the fabric of time vibrated for several long moments then went still. Zordana brought her shaking hands up to her ashen face. The truth of Suh's grave blunder formed in her mind.

"*Fool*! You not only managed to miscalculate the Unspeakable but thrust yourself and three people into the far past!"

Zordana crossed her arms while staring at the ruin around her. The possibility of the four changing the future was very high, even if they figured out where and when they were. That included the wraiths' future as well. She was powerless to undo the damage. The wraith pressed her lips together; she looked toward the Elven city. Returning to the Wold and hoping for a good outcome was not an option.

"Ceela?"

There was no answer. Exhaling slowly, she headed toward Bystyn. The wraith had just cleared the tree line when an Elven patrol galloped toward her. One of the elves raced in her direction while motioning for the others to continue to investigate the billowing smoke.

"You there!"

Zordana stopped and waited for him.

"Do you know what happened here?"

"Yes."

"You'll ride back to the city with me."

The elf held out his hand and, after hesitating for a moment, the wraith jumped up behind him.

Zordana clung to the elf's waist as the horse sped toward Bystyn. Suh managed to collect and mix the right ingredients for the Unspeakable...including obtaining Demon's Breath. None of those that she could see through the window even remotely resembled a demon. Zordana replayed the last few minutes before the explosion in her mind. Most of the action was between the necromancer and her sister's killer. Nothing happened until the murderess raged at the necromancer. Then the Unspeakable reacted. Zordana carefully revisited every step with the outcome pointing to the same conclusion: the murderess was a demon. Wielding magic. The mate of the bearer of the Elven magic. Zordana laughed inwardly at her theory. How preposterous! The Elven magic would *never* tolerate a demon! But this bearer not only accepted the demon but had offspring with it.

A group of riders approached them from the city. The elf reined in his horse as Styph and Seven advanced. Several Elven guards and Herkahs surrounded them.

"What's going on?" demanded the crown prince.

"I don't know. Some of my men are assessing the situation as we speak."

"Who's behind you?"

"A survivor," replied the guard. "She claims to have witnessed the explosion."

"Show yourself. Who are you?"

The wraith peered around the elf. "I am Zordana."

Styph studied her. "What were you doing there?"

"Spending the night."

There was something about the woman that unsettled him. Styph glanced at the dissipating smoke then back to her. "Bring her to the king. *Altyk.*"

The elvish word for 'caution' resonated in the guard's mind as he brought his charge into the city. He raced up the main avenue past people watching the black smoke rising in the distance. They parted to let the speeding horse pass. The elf halted in front of the castle entrance. He helped her down and then escorted her inside. Gripping her thin upper arm, he spoke to the nearest guard in the elvish tongue. The guard hastened to the king's chamber; the elf remained with Zordana near the door.

The wraith struggled to remain stoic even though the mortal's touch repulsed her. A guard motioned for them to continue; with his hand still around her arm, the sentry led her to the king's room. Her identity, she knew, would have to be revealed to the mortals.

Alyxandyr, the Herkah couple, Danyl, and Mason waited for the stranger to be escorted into the king's chamber. The Herkahs's and Danyl's eyes widened with disbelief when she entered the room.

"Abby? It cannot be!" exclaimed Danyl in shock.

"I am *not* Abby," the wraith retorted in a contemptuous voice.

"Who are you then?" demanded Alyxandyr.

"Another wraith," Zada answered for her.

The king's guard surged forward; Alyxandyr lifted his hand to stop them.

"Why are you here?" questioned the Elven king.

"Because Suh made a grave error."

"Explain."

Zordana gazed with disdain at the mortals. "He attempted to create the Unspeakable, but something went wrong."

Alyxandyr looked out the window toward the smoke still rising in the south. "An understatement at best."

"There were three who his blunder sent into the distant past…three who must return with him before they alter the present."

"Who are they and why were they taken by Suh?" inquired Danyl. An uneasy feeling began to grow in his mind.

"A man, an elf woman, and the one who murdered my sister. Suh unintentionally tapped into the very thing he needed to unleash the Unspeakable."

The friends exchanged at first curious then anxious glances.

"And that was?"

"Demon's Breath, Bearer."

She locked gazes with Danyl; he held it until she looked away.

"Find Ramira, Wil, and Hanna," ordered Alyxandyr to the guards stationed at the door. "This had best not be a trap, Wraith."

"I prefer that you address me as 'Zordana'."

"Why are you here, *Zordana?*"

"Because, Elf King, the wraiths are as vulnerable to the four changing the past as you all are."

"She's right," confirmed Zada. "Why were you there, Zordana? What was your part in all of this?"

"I wanted to watch Suh destroy himself. And *her.*"

"It didn't quite work out the way you wanted it to, did it?"

"No, Elf King," she replied in a disappointed tone.

The expressions on the allies' faces ranged from distrust to contempt. The wraith remained standing with crossed arms and scorn radiating from her eyes.

Four wraiths, thought Zada, *two of which had good souls while the spirit of the other one was steeped in evil. This one has swallowed a great deal of pride in coming here, but she does nothing to veil her hatred for mortals.*

"Why do you despise us so?" asked Alyxandyr.

"The Wold suffered from the moment your kind entered it. Three of my sisters are dead because of you mortals."

"Zulant chose to confront that which she could never control," stated Allad.

"My sister would have triumphed had it not been for the

murderess's trickery!"

"Your sister almost unleashed the demons upon the land," explained Allad. "Even the Strait of Sorrows would not have been a sufficient barrier against the Brethren."

Keeping her face unreadable, Zordana studied those gathered. The possibility of the demons wreaking havoc on the Wold was something she had not anticipated. "Zulant's hold over them would have prevented that."

"You're wrong," countered Danyl.

"I think not, Bearer."

"Zulant was never meant to lead them."

"Then who was, Bearer?"

They watched the guard enter the king's chamber, the uneasy look on his face bearing bad news. Alyxandyr's features reflected the words whispered into his ear and were heightened when he read aloud the note the guard handed to him.

"'I have Wil and the woman. If you want to see them alive again then meet me at the tavern a half hour south of the city. Come alone or they die.'"

"Where did you get that from?"

"It was on your kitchen table."

"I believe," Zordana began in a haughty tone, "that was meant for *you*, Bearer."

"Ramira must have found it after I left this morning," said Danyl.

"We all know she would have gone after them," said Allad.

"All three are confirmed missing and, presumably, where Zordana has indicated," confirmed Mason.

"How do we get them back?" Danyl asked, looking at Zordana.

"The murderess protected herself and the others with her magic, which is why they survived the blast. Suh's inability to control the Unspeakable and her power redirected the outcome of the spell."

Danyl bristled when Zordana referred to Ramira in that way. "How do we get them back, Wraith?"

"They have to figure that out, Bearer."

"What is your part in all of this?" asked the Elven king.

"To ensure that the Wold endures."

EIGHT

Suh rolled onto his back and stared up into the leafy canopy. Struggling to regain his senses, he recalled the last few minutes in his mind. The woman not only housed magic but was also a demon. *Da demon will find ya 'fore you find it,* rattled around in his mind. Extreme pain forced the necromancer to sit up. With shaking hands, he pulled apart the remaining strands of material around his upper thigh. The necromancer examined the nasty burn inflicted by the wraith blood. It was not his only injury. Suh gingerly reached up to his throbbing forehead and winced. His fingers stuck to the tacky blood around the gash. Looking down, he spotted a rock smeared with his blood. Suh labored to his feet then leaned against a tree as the landscape reeled around him. The necromancer vomited then wiped the spittle away with the back of his hand. He spotted the vial a few feet away and limped over to pick it up. It was cold to the touch.

Suh scanned the glade. The inn was gone. Did he destroy it when he unleashed the Unspeakable? The dense woods, however, showed no signs of damage. Suh headed in the general direction of the Elven city. He hobbled along for several miles yet the trees never thinned out. How far into the forest was he? He continued on and, just as the sun hovered over the horizon, emerged onto the plains. Another vast tract of trees stretched for untold miles to the east and west, but the city was nowhere to be seen. Exhausted from his efforts, the necromancer searched for a place to spend the night. He crawled beneath a thicket and closed his eyes, the agony on his thigh and aching head his only companions.

Dull pain woke him the next morning. Irritable and hungry, the necromancer staggered to his feet and looked around. The sound of running water urged him to quench his thirst. He ambled over to the river and knelt along its bank. The cold water felt good against his heated forehead and soothed his dry throat. The water did nothing to appease his gurgling stomach. Suh decided to walk toward the orchard to the east. The necromancer plucked and bit into an apple. He scavenged about and found a hazelnut tree. Suh devoured the fruit and nuts. Full for the time being, the necromancer pondered his predicament.

Suh had no clue as to where he was or the whereabouts of the others. He had wraith blood but no potions. His chances of survival without supplies or weapons and in his poor condition were minimal at best. The pirate and the women had to be in the area. Suh needed to find them, but what would he do once he did? He would be at their mercy without any concoctions. The necromancer bit his lower lip in thought. Perhaps there were other people living in the vicinity…individuals who would help a desperate man in need. "Or kill me."

Suh focused on Ramira. The woman's magic intrigued him, especially considering that she was also a demon. And that she and the elf were a couple. The necromancer picked up one of the rocks he had used to crack open the nuts. Tapping it rhythmically on the flat stone, he stared at it unblinkingly. Could he combine the wraith blood with her power?

"Three against one, and she is quite adept at wielding those knives. How would I even take the magic from her?"

He continued striking the rock on the boulder. Sighing heavily, he flung it into the woods. Suh undid the soiled cloth binding his wound. Heat radiated from the blackened edges; a dull, burning pain spread outward from the injury. He focused his attention on the terrain. The leaves retained their green hues yet hints of yellow, red, and orange could be discerned in the foliage. No one moved in the vicinity. His familiarity of the land was limited and the expanse around him did not resemble what he remembered. Elven guards should be patrolling the plains; farmers should be harvesting their fields. Where were they? Where were all of the houses and animal enclosures? The necromancer searched his memory for anything that could help him out of his dilemma. His mind remained blank; his body continued to ache. The sun hung directly overhead. Suh gorged on more fruit and nuts, drank his fill, and then headed in a southwesterly direction.

~

The lead elf glanced over his shoulder at the thousands of elves trudging eastward. He estimated that it had been more than two months since they abandoned their seaside city. Ruled by a select group of elite families, Wyndward's once relaxed and profitable atmosphere was being choked by the council members. Their desire for power had eaten away at the freedoms the elves had long enjoyed. He had confronted them on many occasions, which only succeeded in him being constantly watched. The elf finally realized that the only way to survive and flourish was to desert Wyndward. There were many who shared his idea. The Elven counsel, he was sure, would judge and then hang him for daring to lead the brightest and hardiest young men and women on a foolhardy trek to nowhere if he returned. Some of the elves had turned back at various stages in their journey, but the vast majority continued on in search of a new place to call home. And he would never forsake his followers or his dream.

The elf surveyed the verdant plains before him. Sunlight glinted off a river farther east; fruit and nut trees were interspersed amongst maples and ash. He glanced toward the majestic line of mountains to the north then at the forest between the peaks and himself. They would, he knew, be teeming with game.

"I know what you're thinking," a woman's voice broke through his reverie.

The elf turned his attention to her. The dark-haired woman slipped her hand in his and squeezed it. He looked into her gray eyes which shone with reassurance even though she, like all of the elves, was exhausted.

"Do you approve?" he asked.

She glanced around at the bountiful landscape and nodded.

"Let's discuss this with the rest of the elves when we make camp."

He watched as one of the scouts approached him. "You found something?"

"Three individuals are heading in our direction."

"Are we finally coming across a settlement?" he asked.

"I don't think so," said the scout in a hesitant tone. "They have no supplies, horses or weapons."

"Explain."

"There are two women and one man and one of the women…."

"What about her?"

"She's an elf."

"Did we lose one of our own?"

"None of our people should be ahead of the scouts."

"How far ahead are they?" inquired the leader.

The scout nodded to the southeast.

"Take me there."

The elf and the scout concealed themselves within a dense group of bushes and watched the trio head in their direction. The scout was correct: one of the three was an elf. They heard snippets of the conversation as they closed the distance between them.

Ramira forgot to breathe as the impact of Suh's mistake settled in her mind. He had somehow transported them back in time. Had using the Source of Darkness been complicit in their dilemma?

Alyxandyr's keen gaze scrutinized her and her companions. She remembered his invitation to join them when she had first met him while Mahn destroyed Thebes. Head east, he had told her, and you'll find us. How was she to explain how she got here ahead of Alyxandyr? Had they already altered the future by coming face to face with him? She could explain that Wil was her brother or one of the Thebans, but Hanna?

Hanna gazed upon the face of a tired and sterner appearing Danyl. She sensed an unidentifiable, palpable energy from him.

"It's good to see that you survived," he greeted.

"The city and most of its inhabitants were destroyed," she replied, struggling to contain her nervousness.

Wil and Hanna exchanged confused looks.

Alyxandyr solemnly nodded. "Please…join us."

"Thank you, but we must continue on our journey."

"To where?"

Ramira opened her mouth, but the lies remained lodged in her throat. Their uneasiness coupled with no supplies was not lost on the elf, whose shrewd scrutiny quickly absorbed the inconsistencies of their situation.

"You three are in trouble, yes?"

Ramira could not meet his gaze. Shadows caused his features to become more difficult to read as the sun dipped low on the western horizon.

"Set up camp at the edge of the trees," Alyxandyr ordered the scout. "Then bring food and blankets back here. Be discreet."

The scout departed, leaving them alone. Alyxandyr studied them. His own clothing, as dirty and threadbare as it was, was woven of linen while theirs was fabricated of a sturdier material. It was double-stitched, too. Their boot styles differed from his as well. Their language sounded more casual.

"Perhaps proper introductions will make everyone feel at ease," he suggested.

Ramira felt as if the air was being sucked out of her lungs.

"My name is Alyxandyr, but I have the feeling you already know that. Since you and I never made our acquaintances known," he glanced at Ramira, "I have to assume you learned it from another source."

Ramira swallowed hard. "I'm Ramira and this is Wil and Hanna."

Alyxandyr considered each of them. Ramira, he knew, was from the doomed city; Wil could possibly be from there, too, but Alyxandyr somehow doubted that. Hanna intrigued him the most, for she was not from among the thousands following him.

Hanna stared at the elf, her mind unwilling to process what her eyes beheld. It was impossible for her to be standing before the first king of the elves. He lived a thousand years ago. She focused on the virgin forest around her, one devoid of any manmade structures or of any proof that anyone had ever been here. Bystyn should be prominently situated on the plains yet was nonexistent. She turned back to the elf. If that was the first king, then how could he possibly recognize Ramira? Her mind shuffled the bits and pieces presented to her, yet the fragments reformed in exactly the same way. Hanna looked at Ramira, whose anxious expression did not alleviate her uncertainties. The magic, she realized, had transported them back in time.

"It's an honor to meet you," Hanna stuttered.

"Why is it an 'honor', Hanna?"

All three abruptly looked away.

"I am the leader of a large contingent of elves and we plan on building our homes in this area. It would be very beneficial to know whether or not we are trespassing on someone else's land."

The trio remained silent. Alyxandyr narrowed his eyes.

"What aren't you telling me?" he pursued. "Are there any dangers that I need to be made aware of?"

Ramira shrugged.

"How did you get here ahead of us, Ramira?"

"I…we were not hindered by such a large group," she lied.

Movement beyond the undergrowth caught the companions' attention. Wil, Ramira, and Hanna held their breath as the elves made camp on the plains. Witnessing history, they stood transfixed by the events taking place less than a quarter mile away.

Alyxandyr saw the wonderment on their faces. It reminded him of the reactions the elves back in Wyndward had when the sea dragons came to mate in the bay every ten years. The dark water glowed and shimmered as the sea dragons sought their mates beneath the full moon. The light spectacle lasted until moonset when the sea dragons returned to the deeper waters. They had not returned for two cycles.

"Alyxandyr?" the scout eyed the strangers while carrying an armload of supplies.

"Hmm? Thank you," he said, taking the items from the scout. "I'll check on everyone once they've set up camp."

The scout nodded and returned to his kin.

"You knew that I…we would be here, didn't you?"

Again, silence.

"You're not supposed to be here, are you?"

"We're lost," Ramira confessed.

"You're free to gather around any of the fires."

"Thank you, but we cannot."

Alyxandyr continued to analyze the strangers. They remained close-mouthed and avoided eye contact. Their unusual behavior intrigued him. "If you need anything, please ask."

Ramira breathed a sigh of relief when the future king rejoined his people. Hanna gaped at the elf's retreating back, a look of sheer incredulity etched on her face.

"Is that really *him*?"

"Yes, Hanna," confirmed Ramira.

"He recognized you…and that means..."

"…that I am a thousand years old," Ramira finished Hanna's sentence.

"How is that possible?"

"It's a long, complicated story."

Wil sorted through the supplies, Allad's revelation concerning Ramira's lineage repeating in his mind. The Herkah revealed her ancestry to him while he tended to Ramira after she defeated the wraith and the Black Queen. His curiosity regarding the details that Allad left out matched Hanna's.

"Please…tell us," pressed Hanna.

"I was born in Thebes," began Ramira after several long moments. "The city was situated at the eastern edge of the Great White Desert. Fountains spouting water lined the grand avenue leading to the palace; palm trees and hardy bushes sporting fragrant flowers provided shade throughout the city. Obelisks decorated with pictures and glyphs displayed Thebes' successes. The rich and powerful consumed what the poor labored to provide them. Those who toiled for the nobility were forbidden to partake of the bounty that they supplied."

"You were one of the underprivileged?"

"I was a member of the royal household, Hanna."

Stunned, Hanna could only stare at Ramira.

"I loathed everything that the aristocracy stood for and spent most of my time with the one woman who loved me in the poor quarter."

Wil and Hanna perceived the restrained anguish that fluctuated across Ramira's face.

"How did you meet Alyxandyr?" asked Wil in a quiet voice.

"Scouts told the Ceraphine about a large group of strangers traveling to the south of Thebes. The Ceraphine's arrogance coupled with the High Priestess's cruelty focused on the elves. I shadowed the elves out of curiosity and then, when the truth about Mahn's craving for the Source of Darkness surfaced, I warned Alyxandyr to get as far away as possible."

"The elves would not exist had it not been for you alerting Alyxandyr," breathed Hanna in awe.

Thebes' violent destruction and the cries of those dying within the conflagration reverberated through Ramira's mind. She fought to keep her tears at bay.

"What happened to Thebes?"

"The same demon that attacked Bystyn destroyed it, Hanna."

"So...how did you end up in the future?"

"Divine Providence, Hanna."

"What other surprises are you hiding?" inquired Wil.

"A few," said Ramira, rubbing her pounding temples.

Hanna turned her attention to the campfires sprouting up on the plains amid the breaks in the trees. She was actually observing the birth of Bystyn. Torn between sheer wonderment at what she was witnessing and reviewing what Ramira had revealed, she brought her knees to her chest in thought and stared into the darkness. She smiled at Wil when he placed a blanket over her shoulders.

He then set about lighting a fire. He swung the makeshift arm holding the still warm pot of stew over it. Stirring the contents of the pan, the brigand thought of the future king encamped less than a hundred yards away. Alyxandyr's resemblance to Danyl was uncanny. The future king exuded a hardness and an underlying courage. The elf's stoic probing was equally thorough. Wil respected his tenacity, a resolve that endured in his descendants a thousand years later. Steam rose from the pot. Wil ladled stew into three bowls and handed one to Hanna and another to Ramira. He broke off chunks of bread and gave them their share.

"You know his curiosity is eating away at him," stated Wil. "He'll be back in the morning. Or sooner."

"The less we reveal to him, the better," cautioned Ramira.

"Maybe he can help us get back?" suggested Hanna.

"With the Green Might?"

"The Green Might was not instrumental in bringing us here, Wil."

"I know, Ramira, but perhaps it can be helpful in getting us back."

Ramira thought of Suh, who was undoubtedly roaming around somewhere in the area. He, she was sure, had no idea who Alyxandyr was and would unwittingly be a force in the future of the elves. And the land.

"We have to find Suh," declared Ramira after a brief silence.

"To kill him?"

"No, Wil," Ramira turned her attention to the brigand. "Four of us went back in time and four of us must return."

"It shouldn't be too hard to find him," he said. "He'll need food and shelter and the elves are his only means for both."

"We have to warn Alyxandyr," declared Hanna.

"We can neither warn him nor go to his camp to keep an eye out for Suh."

"So we have to hunt for the little bastard," interjected Wil.

"I hope he didn't bring any extra potions with him," said Hanna.

Wil thought back to the moments prior to their transport. The necromancer's supplies were on a table. Wil closed his eyes and pushed his memory back to when Ramira confronted the necromancer. Suh had reached into his pocket and pulled out a vial of wraith blood. Slipping it back into his trouser pocket, the necromancer's attention was drawn to the effervescing potion in his hand.

"Wil?"

Ramira's voice jerked him back to the present. "All he has is a small bottle of wraith's blood."

The sequence of events formed in Ramira's mind, too. The uncorked vial of wraith blood was poised over the opening of the other ampoule. Something ignited that phial and sent an ominous cloud toward the ceiling. Suh corked the vial of wraith blood and stuffed it into his pocket. The Source of Darkness erupted and surrounded the three of them. The necromancer lunged forward and was also encapsulated within the magic. A brief, white hot light burst. Then they were here. She sighed heavily.

~

Alyxandyr and Annal walked into the center of the group. The elves ceased their conversations and other preparations for the evening. They formed a circle around the couple and, except for an occasional cough or a crying child, everyone was silent.

"We have traveled a great distance to find a new home," commenced Alyxandyr. "Here," he waved all around them, "is everything that we could possibly need. I ask you if you agree and consent to building our new home here. Decide amongst yourselves as to how we should be governed. You do not need to supply an answer right away."

The couple patiently waited while the elves conferred with one another. It didn't take long for almost all of them to approve his choice. The decision was made and, after a long and perilous journey, the elves finally breathed a collective sigh of relief. Not everyone, however, was in agreement. A sullen elf with dark hair and eyes approached Alyxandyr.

"A moment, Alyx?"

The elves wandered out of earshot.

"What's on your mind, Flyn?"

"Will you appoint yourself the supreme ruler or set up a counsel like we had in Wyndward?"

Flyn's directness was not unexpected. His misgivings about the trek eastward became more pronounced during the last few weeks.

"I will let everyone here decide that."

"What if they choose another counsel?"

"Then we will assemble one that does not tear away at our freedoms," replied Alyxandyr.

Flyn mulled over Alyxandyr's words; his face displayed suspicion.

"What else is troubling you, Flyn?"

"That you'll become king and reign with an iron hand."

"Do you actually think that I convinced our kin to travel all this way just to crown myself king?"

"Didn't you?"

Astonishment flowed across Alyxandyr's features.

"Your family was forced to resign from the counsel decades ago and they still live with the shame of their deed. You knew that you had absolutely no chance of regaining your family's honor if you stayed in Wyndward! Coercing our kin to trek away from Wyndward's influence allows you to complete that ultimate objective."

"My grandfather refused to support handing over the majority of the counsel's power to one family." Alyxandyr kept his voice even. "That is nothing to be ashamed of!"

"That created quite the rift, didn't it?"

Alyxandyr's face was livid even though his tone remained calm. "And look how that turned out, Flyn. That family succeeded in acquiring all the power and proceeded to strip us of our individual rights."

Flyn glared at Alyxandyr, who spoke with a conviction steeped in truthfulness.

"If the elves select you as king, then I and many others will leave."

"That is your prerogative, Flyn."

The elves held each other's gazes for a brief moment before Flyn walked away.

Alyxandyr strolled around the perimeter of the camp, helping where needed and offering encouragement to everyone he spoke with. His mind, however, was filled with the three strangers and his heated exchange with Flyn. Both thoughts vexed him. He finally sat down next to Annal and ate.

"The scouts report that there is plenty of food in the area," she said. "The soil is fertile, and there are plenty of creatures we can hunt in the forest and fish in the river. This was a good choice, Alyx."

"Yes, it was," he stated quietly.

"What's bothering you?" she asked after several moments.

"Nothing."

"You're a terrible liar, Alyx."

He offered her a slight smile then continued to eat without tasting a bite.

Wearied from their long march, yet excited about their future, the elves slept soundly. Alyxandyr meandered through the multitude as he did every night. He kept looking toward the three individuals who more than piqued his interest. The lone woman who had urged him and his people away from the destruction in the desert just happened to be in the very spot the elves chose for their home. An elf accompanied her, one that did not belong to the huge group sleeping all around him. Their clothing was different as was the curious response he elicited in all three of them...especially the elf. The man enthusiastically recognized him as someone named 'Danyl'. Ramira had quickly corrected him, so she, too, knew this 'Danyl'.

It's an honor to meet you, echoed in his mind.

"Why?" he whispered into the night.

~

Suh spent an uneventful day searching for another human. His night, he surmised, would be spent in a chilly silence. Returning to the river, he ate and then sought to retain as much warmth as possible. He brought his knees to his chest and fell into a fitful sleep. He woke near midnight and abandoned his shelter. Stretching his cramped muscles, the necromancer surveyed the gloom. He rubbed his arms and turned to go back to sleep when a faint glow to the southwest caught his attention. Firelight. No…many fires. Suh grinned and nodded his head.

"Where there are campfires, there are people. Perhaps I'll introduce myself to them tomorrow."

~

Crickets chirped and creatures moved around in the darkness seeking food. The elves lay encamped less than a quarter of a mile away. Ramira added more wood to the fire and watched Wil and Hanna sleep across from each other. They should, in her opinion, be snuggled up to one another.

Her thoughts turned to Suh. He had latched on to her leg and was transported here with them. The necromancer lurked somewhere in the land and it was up to them to keep him away from the elves. The thought of the necromancer interfering made her very nervous. Suh could change the future in ways she did not even want to imagine. Ramira drank from a water skin then listened to the night around her. She reached for her knives when a rustling sound grew louder. The firelight illuminated Alyxandyr's face; Ramira sheathed her knives.

"What happened after you fled back to your city?" he whispered sitting down beside her.

"I was able to help some of my people to safety."

"I'm glad that some did survive."

The darkened forest was replaced with a city engulfed with flames. The wind whipped up by the inferno drifted toward her, carrying with it bright orange embers and the stench of death. The intense heat caused even the mighty granite walls to crack. The demon Mahn was

nowhere in sight as she searched through the rubble for any survivors.
Stunned Thebans, covered in soot and blood, crowded together near
the edge of the city. Bereft of family, friends, and possessions, these
men and women would assume a nomadic life and become the
Herkahs.

"Why are you *here*, then?"

His voice brought her back to the present. "I can't tell you."

"The only thing I'm sure about you is that you'd be with your
people and not here were it not for some peculiar set of
circumstances."

"Does your mind ever stop processing information?"

"No."

Ramira stared at her clasped hands.

"Who's 'Danyl'?"

Ramira's wistful smile was filled with love.

"Your mate," he guessed.

"Yes."

"Who resembles me?"

"Yes," she confirmed and immediately regretted taking his bait.

"How can an elf be your mate, Ramira, if this is your first time
here?"

Wil rolled onto his back and started to snore; Hanna twitched a
couple of times then settled down again.

"Why are you here?" he persisted.

"I cannot tell you."

Alyxandyr turned her face to his. The uncertainty in her eyes was
not steeped in duplicity but rather in fear.

"Please don't ask any more questions," she begged.

You were here before we arrived. Your mate is an elf and an elf
who does not belong to our group is traveling with you and a strange
man. You have no supplies and, other than your knives, have no other
weapons. Your clothing is different and you already knew who I was.
You refuse to answer any questions and are keeping your distance
from the elves. Alyxandyr's thoughts swirled within his mind. Nothing

made any sense.

"I had two older brothers whom I wanted to be with all the time," said Alyxandyr in a reflective voice. "They, of course, didn't want a little boy trailing after them. So, I decided that I was going to prove how brave I was and they would have to accept me into their circle."

Ramira looked at the elf. Alyxandyr's elbows rested on his thighs. "And that was?"

"There's a spit of land that is exposed during low tide and at its very edge is a pinnacle of rock. During the early spring, fog rides in on top of the waves when the high tide surges in. Hazy clouds would blot out the sun until you couldn't tell which way was up or down. Spring is also the season that the rock sharks mate in those waters."

Ramira's nightmare briefly flared in her mind. Its similarity to Alyxandyr's account was chilling.

"I spent hours atop that rock while the sharks thrashed within the bay. A dorsal fin occasionally broke through the soupy haze. I could discern numerous individuals along the shoreline and hoped that they were witnessing my bravery. I shivered from the cold and damp and, once the tide receded, headed back to shore."

"Did they celebrate your courage?"

Alyxandyr chuckled. "My brothers scolded me and slapped the back of my head while dragging me to face our parents. I wasn't allowed out of the house for a month."

"But you proved your point."

"I did, but it changed nothing."

"I believe it did, Alyxandyr."

"How so?"

"You've navigated past even greater obstacles by leading your people to this place."

Alyxandyr considered her words. An enigmatic force compelled him on this journey into the unknown. The trek east was arduous at best and challenged every soul encamped on the plains. They narrowly escaped certain disaster because the woman sitting beside him had warned them of the dangers occurring in her city. He inhaled deeply and then turned his attention to Ramira.

"Do you believe in fate?"

"Don't you, Alyxandyr?"

Standing up, he turned to her. "I do now."

Ramira smiled as the darkness swallowed him up.

NINE

Sul-Tak eyed the tiny pinpoint of light visible within the oppressive murkiness of the mountain. Too long had the Brethren been imprisoned within the stony crypt, but the end was near. His thoughts returned to Mee-La. The Brethren had offered her their undying allegiance, yet she had not only disregarded their loyalty but had the audacity to align herself with the mortals.

Sul-Tak fingered the Ankh-Nam stuffed in his pocket. She would never again defile the precious amulet. He frowned, for the talisman was created for the very one who had cast aside her heritage. The Vox pulled out the necklace and held it in front of his face: the black facets glittered even in the near lightless cavern. The powerful talisman was useless to anyone but Mee-La, the very individual whom he vowed would never touch it again. The Brethren, he realized, *needed* the Black Queen. She, however, declared the Brethren her enemy. The Black Queen would never willingly place the Ankh-Nam around her neck and allow the power to infuse itself within her soul again.

"Unless, of course, the mortals were at risk," he wheezed to the amulet.

Sul-Tak pursed his lips in thought. A surprise attack on the mortals by the Brethren could force Mee-La's hand, especially if those closest to her were in danger of joining the dark brotherhood. Foremost on that list would be the Herkahs, especially since they were actively involved in slaying the Brethren. She was enamored with the elves and the dwarves, too. A plan began to formulate in his mind, one that would make Mee-La rethink her abandonment of her kind.

~

The friends sat around the table reviewing what the wraith had revealed.

123

"Is she telling the truth, Zada?" asked the Elven king.

"I'm afraid so."

"Can you 'see' them?"

"No, Alyx."

"Why does Zordana despise us so?" Clare asked.

"Ramira slew her sister Zulant and Suh drained her other sister of her blood," clarified Danyl. "She has every reason to despise us."

"But Ramira was in the right and Suh was in the wrong," objected Mason.

"It doesn't matter to Zordana." Danyl stood and walked toward the window. "To her, both were murdered by mortals." *As was Wil's mother.*

"I believe her regarding the possibility of a changed future," stated Zada.

"But they haven't," said Allad.

All eyes focused on the nomad.

"We're still here and nothing has changed," he explained.

"They remain in the past, Allad," Alyx reminded him, "and are still capable of somehow altering the future."

"If they realize where...when...they are they will take every precaution to prevent that from happening."

"We do not know what perils they might face, Allad," said Zada. "Everything could change in the blink of an eye."

Danyl picked up his goblet and walked out onto the balcony. The cool air felt good against his heated skin. He inhaled deeply and then leaned against the balustrade. A dog barked in the distance; a pair of guards patrolled the gardens below him. He ignored the muffled conversations in the room. Questions arose in his mind. How far in the past were they? Were they in any danger? Would they know how to return to the present? What if their attempts to come back thrust them far into the future or shy of the present? What if they never came back?

"Danyl?"

The Elf prince turned to Sophie.

"Why don't I bring the children to my home?"

Danyl pressed his lips together in thought. He preferred that they remain in the castle, but the thought of the wraith's proximity to Kayla and Wyl made him uneasy. He reluctantly nodded. Danyl watched Sophie rearrange the shawl to accommodate both of his children and then carry them out the room.

~

An Elven patrol surveyed the plains a half mile east of Bystyn. The sun's rays penetrated the grayish clouds forming in the sky. The guards pulled their cloaks more tightly around their bodies to ward off the chill in the air.

"When was the last time anyone saw anything move along the edge of the forest?" asked the lead elf.

"Not for a while," replied one of his companions.

The captain glanced up at the empty sky. The gray clouds began to thicken; the sun appeared like a watery disk behind them. His horse snorted nervously; its ears twitched. An uneasy feeling began in the back of the elf's' mind.

"Increase the distance from the tree line," he barked to the others.

The elves galloped a half mile away from the edge of the forest yet even this gap did nothing to alleviate his anxiety. He stopped and waved his men on. Twisting around in his saddle, the elf concentrated on the shadowy woods. Nothing moved nor made any sound. He shook his head and was about to join up with his men when he noticed movement within the trees. Tempered by extreme caution, the captain trotted toward his men without ever taking his eyes off the forest. The shadows finally poured out from underneath the canopy.

"Sweet Mercy!" breathed the captain as the Kreetch continued to swarm out onto the plains.

Racing at full speed, the captain caught up with his men and frantically pointed toward the city. Angling toward Bystyn, the guards watched in horror as the demon horde launched itself at and scrabbled up the gray walls. They continued to climb regardless of the arrows cutting them down. First one, then dozens hauled themselves over the rampart. Sunlight glinted off swords; the wind carried the screams out to the riders. A knot of Kreetch spotted the patrol and surged in their direction. The elves cringed when the city gates slammed shut.

"What are your orders, sir?" yelled out one of the elves.

Survival was their only option.

"Into the woods!" he shouted, guiding his horse toward the trees south of the city.

The elves kept looking over their shoulders and prayed that the loathsome creatures were not in pursuit. They knew all too well what would happen if the demons caught up with them.

~

The chamber fluctuated before Zada's eyes until she found herself in a murky glade surrounded by ancient trees. Long strands of moss hung like tattered curtains from the branches. Glass orbs pulsating with a soft light floated over a slab of black granite balanced on a finger of rock. Zada approached the stone and stared at the threadlike veins of silver drifting upon its surface. She cautiously reached out to touch the surface when a voice called out in warning.

"Do not touch the Wellspring unless you wish to remain here forever."

A tall, thin figure approached her from the other side of the stone table. The hovering lights ignited the tiny silver sparkles in the hood and cloak that concealed its appearance.

"I am Zimun. You are Zada the Seer."

Zada nodded. "What is the Wellspring, Zimun?"

"It is what gives you the sight."

"I don't understand."

"Look upon its surface and tell me what you see."

Zada gazed at the granite's fluid movement and the thin, silver veins drifting upon it. Darker sections speckled with glittering silver points of light emerged and then disappeared into the depths. The nomad held her hand over the stone and felt the sudden rush of cold air that accompanied her into the in-between place. Confusion morphed into uncertainty.

"I'm a wraith?" asked Zada in a small voice.

"No, you are not, but the one to whom you owe your allegiance is a member of the Sisterhood."

"The Lady of the Sand?"

"Yes."

It never occurred to Zada that the Lady of the Sand was a wraith. Zada thought of the arduous ritual she had endured to become the leader of the Herkahs. The stressful ceremony unlocked her inner sight and allowed her access to the gloomy corridor separating the living from the dead. It had also permitted her to travel back in time with Oma. The Lady of the Sand's power originated, so it seemed, from the Wellspring.

Zimun lightly ran her index finger across the Wellspring's surface. Zada watched the silver filaments transform into glittering whirlpools and then separate again.

"Only a wraith can reach into that ultimate darkness, Zada."

"Why am I here, Zimun?"

"Fiendish souls are on the verge of infecting the land." Zimun's husky voice filled the glade.

"Are you referring to the Brethren?"

"They must be stopped."

"Can Zordana help us?"

The wraith cocked her head to the side.

"Zordana is a wraith, is she not?"

"She is a member of the Sisterhood, yes." A hint of displeasure laced Zimun's words.

Zada opened her mouth to speak but the sudden tremor vibrating through the clearing stilled her tongue. Ripples swelled across the hard surface of the slab and splashed over the edges. The ground on which the mysterious liquid landed steamed and hissed. The quake ended as abruptly as it began. The nomad took a step back and looked to Zimun for an answer.

"They have crossed back," said the wraith in a hushed voice. "You must go."

The Wold dissolved, leaving Zada back in the room with her friends. The nomad glanced around the chamber. Allad was in deep conversation with Alyxandyr and Seven while the rest formed loose groups. There was no hint of panic. Did the quake only resonate within the Wold? Zada shoved her thoughts to the back of her mind when Zordana was escorted into the chamber.

"You'll forgive us if we do not quite trust you," began Alyxandyr. "What assurance do we have that you are telling the truth?"

"As I have said before, Elven King, the Wold will suffer if the four change the past."

Zada studied the wraith's reactions. There was a dismissive quality to her words and actions. That coupled with the less than encouraging response from Zimun, left her feeling more than a little concerned.

Running and shouting outside in the hallway halted the discussion. Those gathered turned toward the door as a guard broke protocol and flung it open without being announced. His face conveyed alarm.

"The demons are swarming onto the plain, my Lord," he stated while the royal guards poured into the room. "Some are already in the city."

Alyxandyr motioned to Allad, Danyl, and Seven. The group followed the guards out to the entranceway.

"Only the Kreetch have managed to climb over the walls, my Lord," continued the elf. "The Radir and Vox remain at the edge of the forest."

They exited the castle and surveyed the bedlam in the square. Elves, dwarves, and Herkahs cut down the Kreetch while the inhabitants rushed about in panic to find shelter. They glanced up at the ramparts where elves emptied their quivers into the unseen foes. Dozens of guards hurried to resupply their comrades with more arrows. Their attention returned to the plaza where several Kreetch launched themselves on a horse and its rider.

Danyl jumped onto the nearest horse and hurried toward the largest knot of demons. He willed the Green Might up from his soul and annihilated the closest Kreetch. The Brethren learned quickly and began to mingle with the mortals for protection. Danyl targeted the exposed demons. He looked up the street leading to his home. Dozens of Kreetch darted in his direction. He looked at Sophie's home. His children were with her and she was alone. Danyl's attention returned to the chaos in the square. He incinerated more demons but did not notice two that latched onto his horse and slashed its hindquarters. The steed tried to kick them off but bucked the elf off instead. The Kreetch swarmed over the horse and then turned toward Danyl.

Sophie scooped up Kayla and Wil and fled up to her bedroom with Blue running alongside. Locking the door, she placed the children on her bed and pushed her bureau against it. Breathing hard, she stared at the door while glass shattered on the first floor. Blue's fur stood on end; her claws dug into the wooden planks. Her deep, threatening growling was interspersed with equally menacing hisses.

Sophie began to shake at the sound of claws scraping up the stairs. Kayla and Wyl screamed for their mother and father. Blue exposed her fangs. Bodies thumped against the door, each hit splintering the wood. The demons' high-pitched whines accompanied each thud. Sophie grabbed the terrified children and backed into the corner, her gaze riveted on the fractured door. It finally gave way.

Sophie gaped in horror at the man-like things covered with matted fur. Claws raked the empty air in front of them; fangs dripped with slobber. The pair entered the room slowly and halted in front of Blue. The cat launched herself on the back of one of the Kreetch and clawed at its throat. The other Kreetch jumped on the bed and prepared to vault upon Sophie and the shrieking children.

Clare, Zada, and Zordana rushed to one of the windows facing the mayhem in front of the castle. The dwarf and Herkah stood horrified by what they saw; the wraith's features were tinged with dread. A high-pitched whining behind them stole their breath. The women and wraith reluctantly turned around to face numerous Kreetch. Their dirty fur was covered in blood; their claws scraped against the stone floor while they advanced. Unarmed and cut off from the rooms in the hall, the trio backed away from the monsters until a wall blocked their retreat.

~

Suh studied the goings on in the camp from behind a wall of bushes. He concentrated on the odd collection of elves near where Bystyn should be standing. None of the faces looked familiar; he did not spot his captives and their rescuer amongst the crowds. Pain radiated outward from his wound; his fingers and limbs grew stiff with cold. The necromancer's head throbbed. Suh brushed away the gunk collecting around his eyes and then pushed his greasy hair back. His bowels objected to his diet of fruit and nuts.

He focused on the nearest campfire. It was no more than twenty feet away and was situated in front of several waist-high boulders. He could use the darkness and the rocks for cover and steal one of the blankets and some food. Suh willed the three elves to leave and allow him enough time to grab what he needed. He waited for nearly an hour before the trio joined another group. The necromancer merged with the vegetation and neared the fire. Squatting behind the boulders, he gauged the distance between himself and the needed supplies. Suh took a deep breath and then casually approached the flames. He crouched beside the crackling flames and sighed as his exposed skin tingled in response to the heat. Suh nonchalantly flipped open the flap on the closest satchel and peered inside. Not finding anything to eat, he grabbed the straps of another pack and pulled it toward him. It held a canteen, half a loaf of bread, a bar of cheese, and some dried meat. The necromancer grabbed one of the blankets and a hooded cloak before disappearing into the night once more.

Suh staggered toward a cluster of giant boulders about a quarter mile away. Placing his precious items within the hollowed-out center, he felt safe enough to build a small fire. He ate sparingly, even though his shrunken stomach growled for more food. Washing his meal down with water, Suh stared at the inky sky crowded with stars. Crickets chirped in the grasses; an owl hooted nearby. A large group of elves were encamped to the southwest, but where were Bloodguard, the Elven woman, and Ramira? Around one of the camp fires? Somewhere in the forest? Did they even survive the blast? Suh ran his fingers over the vial in his pocket before falling into a fitful sleep.

~

Alyxandyr lay upon his blankets. Cradling his head in his hands, he looked up into the star-encrusted heavens. The elf pulled his blanket up and tucked it along both sides of his neck. Alyxandyr remembered traveling north along the coastline to the edge of the massive mountain range a few years back. Snow blanketed the country; trees - except for the pines - were without leaves. He sensed the same shift in weather in these parts. Their survival would be brief if they did not erect suitable structures against the cold that seeped down from the mountains to the north. Their existence, he realized, hinged on their ability to adapt to this environment. Used to the balmy weather along the western coast, the elves steadily adjusted to the fluctuating climes along the way.

Tomorrow the elves would harvest as much food as they could. He would send hunters out for game while the remaining elves would chop down trees and build temporary shelters to house his people. Their first year here would try even the hardiest soul. He glanced at Annal as she slept peacefully beside him. He reached out and gently pushed a lock of her hair from her forehead. He placed his hand on her slightly distended stomach and smiled. Their child would be born in the early spring. Alyxandyr snuggled closer to Annal and kissed her cheek. She stirred but did not awaken.

~

Suh flipped the hood up to ward off the early morning chill while he watched the elves from a discreet distance. The other three, he was sure, must be somewhere within the thousands moving about. Elves armed with axes and saws chopped down trees; hunters armed with bows and arrows disappeared into the forest. Dozens of elves filled their baskets with fruits and nuts while others dangled fishing poles on their shoulders heading to the river.

The industrious elves managed to erect the framework for a large shelter by the time the late afternoon sun dipped toward the horizon. Piles of beams and planks grew alongside the structure. Frames holding venison and gutted fish were situated over fires and enclosed with hides; everyone contributed to the settlement.

The light breeze brought the aroma of simmering stew up to his hiding place. The necromancer stood and painfully stretched, his gaze never leaving the bustling scene below. He lit a small fire. Hanging a pot he stole from the camp on a crude arm, he filled it with water and then held his hands over the flames. Despite his magic, there was nothing he could do about the festering wound on his thigh.

~

"We have to search for him," stated Ramira.

"He could be anywhere."

"Then we'll start here and continue outward until we find him, Wil."

The trio broadened their hunt for the necromancer as the day wore on. Their southerly route shifted to the north and then eastward with no results. The sun cast long shadows from the west when the exhausted friends returned to their camp. Sharing a meal, they remained lost in their thoughts. A cold wind seeped into their shelter when the sun disappeared beneath the horizon. Huddled around the fire, Wil, Hanna, and Ramira sat with their blankets draped across their bodies. Suh, they realized, would probably be doing the same thing. Ramira stood and then grabbed a canteen.

"Where are you going?" asked Hanna.

"I'm going to look for a lone fire."

Ramira headed north toward the plains in search of a faint glow. The night was frosty; pitch-black shadows punctuated the gloom as she cautiously crossed the plains. The forest to the north was impenetrable. Silence pressed down on the plains. She glanced to the left and was able to discern the glow of the Elven campfires. Suh would be drawn to them. Ramira pressed her lips together in thought. His confusion would temper any irrational attempts to confront the elves. His need for food, however, would encourage him to test the elves' periphery. Ramira studied the faint lights for several long minutes.

"What would I do if I were alone in a strange place?"

She turned her attention to her murky surroundings. The friendless background sent a shiver up her spine. The necromancer would be forced to seek out other individuals. Ramira headed north searching for that orange pinpoint of light that would lead her to Suh.

~

Unable to sleep, Alyxandyr strode along the camp's perimeter. Except for an occasional hooting owl or the diminishing cricket chirps, the night remained still beneath a quarter moon. He listened to updates from the guards patrolling along the edges. Alyxandyr neared his blankets but sleep still evaded him. For a brief moment, everything became very quiet. Straining his hearing, Alyxandyr detected a faint huffing sound followed by a barely noticeable growling. The disturbance originated a little farther east. Alyxandyr's senses probed the darkness. The subtle din took on definition. Wolves. He was about to yell an alarm when the sentries' shouts broke through the quiet.

The elves grabbed their weapons; torches were lit. Within minutes the entire camp was outlined by fire. The elves peered into the gloomy night searching for the wolves. They did not have long to wait. Glowing yellow eyes drifted along the periphery as the wolves padded back and forth, searching for the easiest attack point. One chose the most direct route and yelped in pain as an elf disemboweled it. The glowing eyes retreated and then returned for a few moments before disappearing into the murky night.

"That was close," breathed the sentry standing beside Alyxandyr.

Deterred by the large group of elves, the wolves crept away in search of easier prey. Alyxandyr squinted into the shadowy night.

~

Hanna and Wil huddled close to the fire. They wrapped their fingers around their mugs for more warmth and wondered how Ramira was faring. Wil readjusted the embers using a branch then placed it on top. The flames crackled to life.

"This is all so surreal," said Hanna.

"I've experienced stranger things," stated Wil, thinking of the Black Queen in Doth-Khan.

"More bizarre than being thrust a thousand years back in time?"

"Yes," he replied adding another piece of wood to the fire.

"Do tell."

"There's a small, rocky island a three-day sail east of Caldon Island that has claimed many ships."

"How so?"

"There are numerous channels in the rocks that, when the wind blows through them from the right direction, sound like women singing. An island full of happy women attracts a ship full of lonely sailors. Unfortunately, the wooden vessels are no match for the sharp rocks submerged below the waves."

"How many ships have been lost, Wil?"

"I think the lesson was finally learned after about four or five vessels," he chuckled.

"Is there anything a man *won't* do to catch the attention of a woman?"

"Probably not."

"How many boundaries do you have, Wil?"

"Three."

"And they are?"

"I refuse to sleep with a reluctant partner nor will I indulge in another man's woman."

"That's only two," she reminded him. "What's the third one?"

"That is something that I'll share with a *willing* partner."

Hanna shook her head and then froze. She held her hand up to quiet Wil and continued to concentrate on the sniffing noises beyond their shelter. The sounds became clearer. Pads snapped small twigs. Low growling. Wolves. Hanna brought her finger to her lips and reached for a branch. She motioned for Wil to do the same. With their backs against a massive boulder, the couple raised the burning wood and searched the darkness. Yellow eyes appeared in the dense undergrowth; high-pitched whining echoed within the glade.

Emboldened by the lack of people, one of the wolves advanced and let out a low growl; its fur stood on end along its back. It skulked around the fire and launched itself at Wil and Hanna. As one, they smashed their branches on top of its head. It lay still for a moment. Wil jammed the brand onto the wolf's back, igniting its fur. It screamed in pain and ran ablaze through the trees. The other predators moved forward and fanned out. The hunt was on.

Wil and Hanna waved their crude weapons at the wolves, but the animals continued to close the distance. Two of the wolves leapt at the pair and fell dead at their feet. Arrows stuck out from their necks. The sudden arrival of elves on horseback scattered the remaining predators. Wil and Hanna nodded in gratitude to Alyxandyr and his men.

"How did you know?" asked Hanna.

"They visited us first," explained Alyxandyr.

"We are in your debt," said Wil.

"Here," stated Alyxandyr, handing them a couple of swords, "you might need these."

"This is very generous of you," said Wil.

"It would be much safer if you joined us."

"That's tempting, but we have to decline," replied Hanna.

"You know where to find us if you change your mind."

Wil and Hanna watched the elves drag the carcasses out into the darkness. The desire to accompany them was overwhelming.

Ramira spent hours along the plains and within the tree line to no avail. Wearied from her efforts, she headed back to camp as the sun's first rays stained the sky with lavender, red, and golden hues. Ramira added more wood to the fire. Steam rose from the pot; the scent of peppermint hung in the air. She offered Wil a tired smile when he sat down beside her. Dark circles accentuated her puffy eyes.

"Anything happen while I was gone?"

"We were attacked by wolves," answered Hanna.

Ramira shuddered. She remembered the wolves that stalked her and Danyl along the Broken Plain. They, too, were almost killed by the beasts.

"If it weren't for Alyxandyr, we'd be quite dead," added Wil.

"I should not have left you two unprotected."

"He gave us these," said Hanna, holding up one of the swords. "We can hold our own the next time you venture out."

Ramira nodded, the effort sapping her of whatever strength she retained.

"You need to sleep," stated Wil.

"He's right, Ramira," added Hanna, accepting a mug of tea. She closed her fingers around the cup.

"I'm fine."

"No," he admonished, "you are not."

"Why don't you try to get a few of hours sleep?" suggested Hanna. "We'll keep watch."

Exhausted, Ramira lay on her blankets. She fell asleep almost immediately. Wil added his blanket and brought the edges up under her chin. Sitting down beside each other, they watched her in silence while sipping their tea.

"Tell me the truth about Caldon Island."

Wil stared into his mug, knowing what answers Hanna sought. He was not proud of his past but felt that she deserved an explanation.

"Daris Haven was a port ruled by a wealthy and influential spice merchant and his family," he began in a voice laced with bitterness. "My mother and I lived on the outskirts. One day two of the spice merchants' sons happened upon our home. They brutalized her in front of me until she died of her injuries."

Hanna looked into his face and, for the first time, saw the raw emotions within it.

"I was only ten years old but vowed revenge on them. I worked my way up until I had amassed enough power and influence to inflict my vengeance. I ordered the spice merchant, his sons, and his business partners hanged then banished his entire family to a distant island in the ocean. Daris Haven became Graveyard and I its supreme leader. Surrounded by wealth and a sense of superiority, I disregarded the morals and emotions my mother imparted to me. I took what I wanted regardless of the consequences. The only thing I would never do is to take a woman without her consent."

"What penetrated into your 'sense of superiority'?" she asked in a soft voice.

"Ramira."

"How so?"

"She was beautiful and dangerous and wanted absolutely nothing to do with me."

"You didn't know that she was Danyl's mate, did you?"

"No."

"So, what happened?" pressed an intrigued Hanna.

"The Healer, Abby, sought a favor from me by allowing her, Ramira, and Allad seats on one of my ships to go back to the mainland. Suh attacked Graveyard and I was imprisoned while they escaped. I eventually fled and headed west."

"To find Ramira."

"To find and punish her," he admitted.

"Why? What did she do?"

"I blamed her for my downfall, Hanna. I spent a year imprisoned in my own building, waiting for the opportunity to seek my revenge on her."

"I don't understand, Wil."

"*I* was my own worst enemy and Ramira unknowingly forced me to face that reality."

"When did you finally acknowledge that?"

Wil stared into his half-empty mug as the precious intimate hours replayed themselves in his mind. His love for Ramira manifested itself in their beloved son and the cherished friendship he now shared with her and Danyl. Those things meant everything to him.

Hanna studied his face, which was filled with an unspoken tenderness and humility.

Wil lifted his tunic and exposed the burn scars. "When, even after Suh did this, I still had to warn Ramira of his presence."

Hanna reached out and lightly ran her fingertips over the scars. "To protect her."

"Yes," he replied. "There are other marks, but I don't feel like dropping my trousers to show you. By the way," he added, "he *missed* the important parts."

Hanna offered him a slightly embarrassed smile while he tugged his tunic back into place.

"I've done a great many things that I am not proud of and that I cannot change, Hanna," he confessed. "All I can do is to be a better man."

Hanna brought her knees to her chest and rested her chin on them, mulling over what he had told her. And what he had not. The aphrodisiac, she suddenly realized, was meant for Ramira. Had he used it? She looked at him and knew he would never betray her.

"How long were you and Ramira in each other's company on Caldon Island?"

"An hour at best."

"Alone together?"

"No, Hanna, amongst dozens."

"That hardly seems like enough time for her to have influenced you."

"It was enough time."

Hanna decided to change the subject. "What about Jules?"

"What about her?"

"Did you ever love her?"

"No."

"What kept you two together, Wil?"

"Ambition and power coupled with our physical needs."

"She was very explicit about that."

Wil faced her. "What exactly are you implying, Hanna?"

Avoiding his gaze, the elf shrugged and looked into her cup.

"You're intimidated by her."

"Yes and no."

"Explain."

Hanna took a deep breath while trying to contain her innermost feelings. "She exudes a sensuality that I…that is undoubtedly beyond my capabilities. I mean *if* we were ever to…share a moment like that."

Wil gazed into her eyes. A flush crept up into her cheeks. "I've learned the hard way that intimacy *without* love leaves you feeling empty inside."

Hanna turned her attention to a slumbering Ramira. She had spent all night searching for the necromancer to keep him from interfering with the elves. Ramira warned the elves even though her own people were being decimated by a demon. Her unflagging loyalty extended beyond just her family and friends. Ramira clung to what she believed was right regardless of the consequences. *Where do you draw your strength from?*

"Is this the kind of 'adventure' you were seeking?"

Hanna shifted her gaze to Wil. "My 'adventure' began the moment you started to pester me at the tavern."

"Is that good or bad?"

"Well, I'm sitting beside a pirate a thousand years in the past with a woman who wields magic sleeping a few feet away. I'm witnessing the birth of my home, and I've been in the presence of the first king on several occasions. I'm filled with both amazement and fear, and I have no idea if we're ever going to get back to our own time. The most excitement provided by a previous suitor was watching him scream like a little girl when a snake crawled up his pant leg during a picnic."

Wil chuckled. "What happened?"

"He dropped his trousers and ran about a mile away while I carried the poor snake to the bushes!"

"So…good or bad?"

Hanna kissed him in response.

~

Ramira's nightly excursions looped around from east to west until it brought her to the outskirts of the Elven camp. Peering through the underbrush, she smiled at the elves' hard work. Alyxandyr and his people managed to erect the frameworks for several buildings; orderly piles of flat boards and sturdy beams were situated by each one. The elves would have durable shelters before the first snow fall. Ramira continued her stealthy search for the necromancer. She followed the edge of the Elven camp north, stopping every few minutes to scan for any signs of a light. Vegetation blocked the flickering firelight leaving her in almost total darkness. Crouching down behind a fallen tree, she spotted a faint light farther to her right. Ramira warily circled around and approached it from the east.

Hiding behind a series of boulders, she saw Suh hunched over beside a small fire. The light reflected off the perspiration on his face; a low moan escaped his lips whenever he moved. A collection of branches and pieces of wood lay in a heap near the fire; several flattened pouches were strewn about. The once fastidious necromancer appeared filthy; dark circles accentuated his pale face. A glass vial sparkled in the firelight beside him.

She watched him shift his blanket with a trembling hand, revealing a scorched section of fabric where his pocket once was. He gritted his teeth while lifting up a piece of material covering an ugly wound. Ramira thought back to when Wil came to her home suffering from the burns inflicted on him by Suh. Wil's agony lasted for days. *How does that feel, Suh?*

The necromancer flinched when she appeared out of the darkness. Ramira couldn't tell if it was due to the wound or her sudden entrance. She hoped it was the former.

"I believe that proper introductions should be made," he said in a pain-filled voice that still dripped with arrogance.

"I know who you are."

"And I know *what* you are."

Ramira stared dispassionately down at the necromancer.

"So…you finally found me. What are you going to do, *Demon*? Kill me?"

"Not yet."

"I must admit that your beauty concealed what was in your heart."

"Get up," she ordered, ignoring his syrupy attempt to distract her.

"It's no wonder that Captain Bloodguard desired you so."

Ramira suppressed the urge to end his useless existence.

Continuing, Suh baited, "He has always had good taste in women…none more so than *you*."

Refusing to fall for his lure, Ramira waved him to his feet.

"What was he like, *Demon*?"

"I'm not going to ask you again!" she hissed through clenched teeth.

"Did he satisfy your every *need*?"

Ramira brought her fist down on his temple; Suh crumpled to the ground. She cut the straps off the pouches, tied them together, and then bound his hands behind his back. Ramira smothered the fire with dirt. She picked up the vial of wraith blood and stowed it in her pocket. Groaning brought her attention back to Suh, who slowly regained consciousness. She stuffed a wad of material into his mouth and then yanked him to his feet.

Breathing heavily, the necromancer limped down the hill. He started to drag his left leg halfway back to the camp. The faint smudges of color in the east heralded the sunrise, which cast long shadows across the plains. Ramira ignored the man's muffled whimpers and pushed him forward. She jerked him to his feet whenever he stumbled.

~

"Ramira should have been back by now, Wil!"

Wil watched the rising sun chase the darkness from the plains. Ramira had been gone the whole night. Was she incapacitated somewhere? Did a predator manage to attack her? Was she lost?

"We should go look for her."

"Where would we start, Hanna?"

"Certainly not here!" she retorted.

He was about to reply when a pair of silhouettes appeared. Wil glared at Suh. The necromancer's ashen face sported a bruise near his temple; dirty fabric was crammed into his mouth. He favored his left leg.

"Where did you find him?" asked Wil.

"Just east of the Elven camp."

The necromancer labored to sit on the ground. Leaning against the tree trunk, he straightened out his legs. The perspiration running down his grimy face left whitish streaks in its wake.

"What's wrong with him?" inquired Hanna.

"He has a severe burn on his thigh."

Ramira unbound the soiled cloth. Suh's wound oozed pus; the swollen redness covered his upper thigh.

"That must be uncomfortable," said Wil with satisfaction.

Suh glowered at him for a moment and then turned his head away.

"We should help him," stated Hanna.

"Like he helped me?"

"That's what separates us from people like him, Wil."

They watched Hanna disappear into the forest.

Ramira grabbed the canteen and crouched in front of Suh. Removing his gag, she poured some water into his mouth.

"Remain quiet or I'll shove this," she held up the material, "back into your mouth, understand?"

Exhausted from the trek to the camp and in too much pain to argue, the necromancer closed his eyes and nodded.

"What vile spell were you trying to conjure up?" demanded Ramira.

"One beyond my capabilities," he confessed in a hoarse voice.

Wil shook his head in disgust then watched Hanna return with a handful of leaves and moss.

"Here," she said, placing a waxy leaf in his mouth. "Chew on this. It'll dull the pain."

Hanna prepared a poultice with the remaining vegetation. She added hot water to the thick mixture and stirred it until it was smooth. Hanna lifted the necromancer's chin and looked into his glazed eyes.

"This will be painful," she cautioned him. She motioned for Wil and Ramira to hold him.

Suh convulsed as the greenish paste made contact with his wound; his screams echoed within the clearing. Tears streamed down his cheeks as the poultice began to bubble.

Wil glared at the man who inflicted that same torture onto him. He saw no sympathy in Ramira's eyes, either. Hanna repeated the application until the mixture ceased foaming. Suh fell into unconsciousness after the first treatment.

Lost in thought, Ramira gazed into the distance. The necromancer's failed spell thrust them into the past. She glanced at his covered wound then removed the vial. She looked at the silvery liquid and then at Suh. Had the flawed potion ignited the wraith blood? Did it react to the Source of Darkness? Or did it have nothing to do with either one?

Ramira thought back to the moments before they were transported back to the distant past. *Suh corked the vial and stowed it in his pocket...her breath ignited the potion in his hands...the men ran for their lives...she grabbed Wil's and Hanna's hands...the Source of Darkness surrounded them...there was an explosion a mere second after Suh latched onto her leg…and then they were here.*

She suddenly realized that the Source of Darkness was protecting them from the disastrous effects of the potion. It flared to life to ward off whatever transpired in the room. It wasn't until Suh made contact with her that the wraith blood ignited. But to what? Her magic? Ramira held up the phial and swirled its contents. She eyed the slowly forming sparkles; heat began to emanate from within. She placed it on the ground and breathed a sigh of relief when the shimmering ceased. Ramira watched Wil pick it up without any reaction to it.

"How did this end up with you?" mumbled Ramira to the motionless necromancer.

"From me," replied Wil.

"Where did you find it?" she asked in a surprised voice.

"Doth-Khan."

Ramira stared at him. "The demon lair?"

"It rolled toward me when…during the battle," he quickly finished.

"Abby had it?"

"Apparently so."

"How did she get it?" Ramira wondered out loud.

"Maybe it's her blood," suggested Wil.

"Why would she carry around a vial of her own blood?"

"If not hers, then whose is it?"

Hanna listened to the conversation - none of it made any sense to her. "Where is this 'Doth-Khan' and what is this 'wraith blood' that you're talking about?"

Wil and Ramira exchanged uneasy glances, for only a handful of individuals knew the truth about the Black Queen's epic clash with Zulant. The Black Queen's identity would remain with those people.

"Doth-Khan was the demon lair in the Great White Desert," clarified Ramira. "It was destroyed and the demons were driven to the other side of the northern mountains."

"What were you doing there, Wil?"

"Being a nuisance," Ramira answered for him.

Hanna knew all too well what the demons were capable of but

Wil's and Ramira's enigmatic relationship intrigued her. Hanna was about to pursue the topic when Alyxandyr joined them. She stifled the urge to bow to him once more.

The elf looked at the prone man who began to stir back to life. He deposited a satchel full of food on the ground.

Suh opened his eyes. The pain in his thigh was reduced to a tolerable aching. He squinted at the stranger standing a few feet away and then recognized him. The elf prince. The bearer of the Elven magic. Standing beside him was his mate…the wielder of another power. Both were within easy reach. Injured, tied up, and bereft of his potions, the necromancer chortled until a coughing fit silenced him.

"What's wrong with him?" asked the elf.

"He just realized that Fate has a wicked sense of humor," stated Ramira dryly.

"And that would be?" he pursued.

"You can't catch a hawk with a butterfly net."

Shaking his head, Alyxandyr crouched next to the semi-conscious man. Lifting up the material, the elf examined the ugly wound. Heat radiated off the injured man; sweat rolled freely down his face and neck. The elves had medicines to help him but Alyxandyr was not about to waste them on a dead man. He glanced up at Ramira and Wil, and noticed that neither showed any concern for the man's agony.

"Who is he?"

"He's the reason why we're here," answered Ramira in bitter tones.

"Where did you find him?"

"Near your camp."

"That explains the missing supplies," he stated.

"We're sorry for any inconvenience that he caused," said Ramira.

"What will you do now?"

"Continue our journey."

"To where?" pressed the elf.

"Hopefully to where we belong," replied Ramira.

Wil, Hanna, and Ramira met the future king's gaze but remained silent. Realizing that they would not be forthcoming with an explanation, Alyxandyr returned to the awakening camp. Movement caught his attention when he emerged from the trees and brush. Several hundred elves headed west. Flyn. The remaining elves had chosen him to be their king; Flyn made good on his promise. Alyxandyr silently wished them well.

Hanna blotted the sweat on Suh's face with a cool cloth; he weakly pushed away the blankets. His damp forehead was hot to the touch; he moaned as the infection spread outward from his wound.

"The treatment was too late," she said. "He's not going to live much longer."

Ramira took a deep breath while watching the necromancer writhe in pain. Wil, too, suffered horribly from the burns courtesy of the man on the ground. There was nothing they could do for the necromancer, whose evil intentions led him to this moment. What if he died before she could figure out how to get back home? Bury his body here in the forest? Take it with them? She held aloft the vial. Was it the catalyst that propelled them back in time?

Ramira's attention was drawn to the crude bandage around the necromancer's thigh. The Source of Darkness reacted to protect them from the blast. The wraith blood responded to her magic by releasing its white-hot energy. Ramira placed the ampoule on a flat rock and sat down in front of it. She willed the Source of Darkness up from the depths of her soul until a slender amethyst tendril appeared at the end of her finger. She brought it close to the vial. The wraith blood began to sparkle. The blood became lusterless when she withdrew her digit. Ramira repeated the motion several times, each with the same result. She looked at Wil, who seated himself beside her.

"You found our way home."

"Or to our deaths," she replied.

"Shouldn't we end up where we began?" asked Hanna in a nervous tone.

"I don't know."

Wil studied Ramira's tense face. "Why were we transported *here*?

What was the connection?"

"Me," she replied.

"And the link to our time?" he continued.

"You, Hanna, and Suh."

"And you, too, Ramira," he reminded her.

Only Suh's raspy breathing broke the silence.

"We have to try," Wil said, taking her hand in his.

"We could all die."

"But we won't."

Ramira nodded and motioned Wil and Hanna to the necromancer's side. They did not need to be told to hang on tightly to each other. Would the wraith blood sear her flesh like it did Suh's or would the Source of Darkness protect her? Ramira took a deep breath and, feeling the secure grip Wil and Hanna had on her, willed the magic to life. The vial's contents glittered for a brief second before a blinding white light spread outward. The resounding explosion ripped through their camp.

Startled by the thunderous boom, Alyxandyr and the elves searched the landscape for its origin. An eerie sensation grabbed hold of Alyxandyr. He headed for the camp in the woods, the thought of something bad happening to the strangers foremost in his mind. He approached their site and inhaled sharply. Charred and splintered trees and scorched earth carved out a huge area where their campfire once stood. A series of boulders now protruded from the ground. They reminded him of a dragon's backbone.

They were immediately propelled into an icy blackness. Lights streaked by and web-like strands burned wherever they brushed against their exposed skin. The arctic air threatened to freeze their lungs. Gooseflesh erupted on their skin; tears streamed from their eyes. A sense of panic terrorized their flagging courage. They instantly lost their sense of direction and slipped into unconsciousness.

Wil struggled to his feet and looked around the glade. The Dragon's Backbone poked out from the ground. A blackened and fractured pit was all that was left of the inn and stables. Suh lay in a motionless heap in its center. Wil knelt beside Hanna. Satisfied that she was unhurt, he searched for Ramira. He glanced at Hanna who knelt beside Suh. She shook her head.

Weakened by her efforts, Ramira rolled over onto her back and stared up at the canopy. The scar from the Ankh-Nam began to prickle then burn. A familiar sensation wormed its way through her mind, one that made her shudder. She staggered to her feet, the look of dread on her face alarming Wil and Hanna.

"Ramira? What's wrong?"

Ramira ignored Wil and lurched toward the plains, the others a step behind her. She regained her strength and began to sprint. Wil clasped Hanna's hand as they ran on. The trees and brush began to thin out and, as they rushed onto the southern portion of the plains, slid to a halt. Forgetting to breathe, all they could do was gape at the demons surging westward toward Bystyn.

A group of riders headed in their direction. Ramira frantically waved them over. The Elven patrol halted in front of them but their attention remained on the Brethren.

"Give me your horse!" demanded Ramira of the closest elf.

She jumped onto its back then turned to the guard. "Keep these two safe!"

Ramira kicked the horse's sides and raced toward the Brethren, heedless of Wil's and Hanna's cries. She glanced to the left and watched with horror as the leading edge of Kreetch tried to climb up Bystyn's walls. Undeterred by the arrows raining down on them, the demons clambered up the gray walls.

Ramira concentrated on the knot of Vox heading toward the city. They stopped when they noticed her riding in their direction. She pulled on the reins, dismounted, and then sprinted on. Ramira identified Sul-Tak and approached him. A number of demons lunged at her only to be incinerated by the Source of Darkness. She saw Sul-

Tak wave them off, allowing her a clear path to him. The whining and snarling faded away.

"Mee-La," greeted Sul-Tak with a mock bow.

Ramira glared at the Vox as he held up the Ankh-Nam. "What do you intend to do with that?" she questioned.

"You will wear the Ankh-Nam and then take your rightful place amongst the Brethren."

"Or what?"

"Or I will order the Brethren to destroy the mortals," wheezed the Vox.

"Your time is almost over, Sul-Tak," she began. "Ush-Tak recognized that."

"Ush-Tak's weakness led to his death, Mee-La."

"Your overconfidence will lead to yours, Sul-Tak."

A glacial fire burned in Ramira's chest. Her nightmare of standing on a pinnacle of rock accepting the Ankh-Nam filled her vision. She stared at the amulet dangling from the Vox's hand and remembered how its power had seduced her. Ramira would not be able to escape its horrifying grip a second time. She watched Sul-Tak close the distance between them. The amulet reflected the diminishing sunlight as dark clouds blotted out the sky.

"Be who you are meant to be, Mee-La."

The closer Sul-Tak advanced, the more excruciating the amulet's scar ached.

"Place it around your neck, Mee-La."

The agony radiated out to her arms and legs.

"Embrace your heritage, Mee-La."

Ramira struggled to breathe.

"Rule the darkness for eternity, Mee-La."

The dark power continued to blister her from within. The Ankh-Nam continued to hang nonthreateningly from the Vox's hand. Ramira placed her fingers on the scar. It emitted a searing heat. Warmth pulsed along her thighs. She slid her knives out of their sheaths and held them in front of her. The markings glowed with an unearthly light. They were meant for her death and the release of the Source of Darkness. Visions of the blank scrolls and unadorned Theban walls filled her mind. The blurry images came into focus. Imhap's lessons echoed in her mind. The symbols took on meaning. She turned the blades and read the inscription:

The death of the One,
By these blades
Shall forever release,
The darkest of shades.

"Take the amulet," Sul-Tak's raspy voice broke the eerie silence.

Terror flooded her being. Understanding supplanted Ramira's panic.

"You are holding nothing more than a useless trinket."

"How dare you insult the amulet!" he roared.

Ramira ripped open her tunic. "*I* dare because I *am* the Ankh-Nam!"

Sul-Tak gaped at the glittering blackness on her chest that sizzled with energy. He looked into her eyes and watched as the blackness displaced the whites and amethysts.

Ramira offered him a contemptuous look. She placed the tips of her blades against the glittering blackness then plunged them in up to their hilts. The symbols along the blades ignited and blazed with an inner fire. The Black Queen's magic flared to life and encompassed her body within a dazzling column of black sparkles. They obscured the advancing Vox and immersed her in a bitterly cold emptiness. Ramira identified the Black Queen's might and sent it out of her body and toward the demons.

Wil gasped then dropped flat on the ground as the shimmering black power erupted from Ramira and sliced into the demons. Piles of glowing ash dotted the plains, forest, and ground around the outer walls of the city. The gleaming black column encompassing Ramira continued to pulse, sending out more rays that sought out and eradicated the demons. He wrapped his arms around Hanna as she, too, witnessed the Brethrens' annihilation.

Ramira struggled to retain her soul while the malevolent energy burst from her body. Every pulse sucked out more of her strength; every strike felt like spikes being hammered into her head. She grasped the hilts, afraid that letting go would not complete her lethal task. She felt the last of the Black Queen's magic leave her body and was finally able to see beyond the swirling evil. The Brethren were gone. She crumpled to the ground. Fine dust and residual magic floated in the air around her. Their objective finally completed, the black blades pulsed once and then vanished. It was done.

"Forgive me," she breathed.

TEN

The Kreetch continued to pour into the city. Danyl grew weak with his exertions. The Green Might's potency dwindled until only sporadic bursts remained. Sensing the loss of power, the demons swarmed around the elf. As one, they pressed closer to Danyl. He scorched the leading edge of the Kreetch until he wielded the last of the magic. Unchallenged, the demons rushed him. Danyl desperately tried to coax the magic back to life, but it refused his command. He took a steadying breath and awaited the inevitable outcome. To his complete shock, glittering black light appeared. He and the other mortals instinctively lay flat on the ground and covered their heads. The snarling and whining immediately ceased.

Sophie clutched the crying babies, her wide eyes focused on the demon that leapt toward them. A black blur intercepted the demon and forced it against the wall. The Kreetch struggled upright and resumed its attack on Sophie. Blue lunged at the demon but the Kreetch was ready for her this time. It raked Blue along her side and then slammed her against the wall. Blue lay still. Enraged, the Kreetch propelled itself at Sophie and the children. A glittering black light incinerated it a split second later.

~

Memories of the Vox attacking them and Cooper filled Zada's and Clare's minds. The surviving Vox from that battle nearly managed to possess Zada, who had stabbed the Vox with her waning courage. This time, however, no help would be forthcoming.

The Kreetch formed a semi-circle and leapt forward. The women brought their arms up and looked away from the horrors about to occur. An unexpected blinding light and accompanying wave of energy forced them to the floor. The ensuing silence urged them to look around. The wind flowing in from the broken window stirred the mounds of powdery residue.

Danyl rose to his feet and stared at the carnage in the city. Bodies of men and animals lay in the street, their blood filling the spaces in between the cobblestones. Breathing hard, the elf signaled to a group of guards. The elves gestured back and, with swords drawn, searched for any remaining demons. His father, Seven, and Allad raced toward him. Danyl waved to them and then raced to Sophie's house, his worst fears playing out in his mind.

"Sophie!"

"Upstairs!"

Danyl bounded up the stairs two at a time then squeezed his way through the splintered door. A shaken Sophie clutched his wailing children. He hugged and kissed all three of them.

"Blue…"

Danyl followed her gaze. Blue mewled softly when Danyl crouched by her side and gently stroked her chin. Blood smeared the wall behind her and pooled underneath her body.

~

Wil sprinted toward the still form at the edge of the forest. Slapping the reins against the horse's haunches, he silently begged that she was still alive. The brigand pulled on the reins and dismounted before the mare came to a complete halt. He crouched down beside Ramira and brushed away the hair covering her face. Blood trickled from her nose and mouth; her eyes were wide open. Her breathing came in short gasps.

"Demons?" she asked in a hoarse voice before coughing up blood.

"Gone…all gone."

"Smash the amulet."

Wil looked around and spotted the Ankh-Nam off to one side. He scrambled over to the amulet. Placing it on a flat rock, Wil grabbed a fist-sized stone and brought it down on the necklace repeatedly. It shattered beneath the impacts until nothing but tiny fragments remained.

"Ramira? Can you hear me?"

"Is she dead, Wil?" Hanna asked in a small, frightened voice.

"Please…say something!"

Ramira stared at the fuzzy shadows before her. Everything appeared indistinct; all sounds were muffled. It reminded her of being submerged in water while looking up toward the surface. The fire in her chest was out. A bittersweet sensation washed over her as she drifted out of the land of light and into the darkness. She floated in the frigid space while the malevolent souls of the Brethren hurtled past her. One soul flowed past her, his face contorted with fear and rage. Suh. The blackness swallowed his soul. She desperately searched the darkness for her children's souls. To her relief, they were not here with her. Ramira encased herself with the memories of her children, Danyl, and all the other people she had loved and then continued on her journey.

~

Zordana picked her way over the bodies. She avoided the elves, dwarves, and Herkahs as they tended to the wounded and collected the dead. Try as she might, she was unable to muster any smug satisfaction for the mortals' calamitous end. Even she had to admit that they fought admirably to protect their own. Zaura had detected the good in their spirits, which allowed her to endure those that exuded bad intentions. Zordana's attention shifted to the Elven king and the other leaders as they helped anyone in need. Their faces reflected the grief that welled up in their hearts for all those slain by the demons. Zordana opened her satchel and mixed her blood with the potions. Kneeling beside the closest injured man, she administered the concoction to the gashes on his chest.

~

Tears streamed down Hanna's cheek as she gazed upon Ramira's lifeless body. She glanced at Wil, who refused to let Ramira go. He pushed away Hanna's hand when she tried to close Ramira's eyes.

"She's gone, Wil," she gently whispered.

"No…she's not!"

Hanna looked up as the Elven guards reined in before them. Wil picked up Ramira's limp body.

"Ride ahead and find Danyl and Zada," he ordered. "Tell them to meet us at his home."

"Wil…."

"She can't be dead, Hanna!"

The Elven guard approached and dismounted. Placing their fists across their hearts, the elves saluted Ramira.

"Let's bring her home, Wil." Hanna's voice was thick with emotion.

Wil climbed onto the back of one of the horses and took Ramira's body from one of the guards. The ride back to Bystyn was a solemn one. The Elven guard rode on either side of Wil; Hanna sat behind one of the elves. They entered the city and were shocked by the slaughter left behind by the demons. Bloody corpses and piles of ash were everywhere. He looked at Ramira's ashen face and tried hard not to imagine how much worse it would have been had she not sacrificed herself. Wil steered the horse toward the house and passed her to one of the elves while he dismounted. The guard led them to the kitchen door and opened it. Wil entered the home and positioned her on the sofa.

Hanna gave Wil a wet cloth and watched as he washed away the blood on her face and neck. The devotion with which he attended Ramira broke Hanna's heart. Would he ever be able to love another woman again? Would he even try? A commotion by the kitchen door broke through her thoughts. She and Wil stood up and made room for the prince on the sofa. Danyl's choked cries as he rocked Ramira back and forth compelled Wil and Hanna to hold each other.

~

Alyxandyr and the other leaders assessed the death and destruction caused by the demons. Standing in the middle of the square, they accepted both verbal and written messages. Tasks were assigned and carried out by elf, dwarf, and nomad. The bodies were picked up and the demon ashes swept up and disposed of.

Few noticed the body of the slight man tied to a horse; only two recognized him. Tong and Jules watched as Suh passed by. Unable to carry out their plan, the pirates concentrated on saving their own lives from the demon attack. Fortune smiled down on them and not Suh. Tong smiled inwardly; Jules reconsidered her plans.

"I suggest that we leave as soon as we get enough supplies," he stated.

"Perhaps we can still salvage parts of the plan," she proposed.

Tong stared at her. Jules' irrational obsession with the elf and Bloodguard had only one outcome, and it was not a good one. Suh was dead and he was finally free. Tong was damned if he was going to waste his time and life pursuing her idiotic plans.

"Why are you looking at me that way?"

"I don't care what you do, Jules, but I'm leaving."

"And go where?"

"Where opportunities are less deadly."

Jules chewed the inside of her cheek in thought. With Suh dead, a new leader could emerge and seize Widows Point and Caldon Island. She had the right skills but needed the right individuals to complete her scheme. Tong's presence would strengthen her claims to be the new leader. Many were loyal to him.

"Jules? Are you coming?"

"Why don't you and I forge a new partnership?"

"I'm not staying here, Jules."

"Not here…back east."

"Widows Point and Caldon Island?"

"Why not?" she replied with a broad smile.

Tong's mind formulated a different plan. "Why not indeed."

The elf king nodded to one of the guards then looked past him at an approaching Wil. Stubble covered his face; his clothing was dirty and torn. The downcast look on his tired and bloody face did not bode well. Alyxandyr felt his chest tighten when Wil stopped before him.

"Hanna and Ramira…."

"Hanna is in the house," he said in a fatigued tone while half-heartedly pointing back the way he had come.

Zada, Allad, the dwarf couple, and Styph joined them, their tentative smiles fading when they saw the look on Wil's face.

"Ramira?"

Wil swallowed hard and shook his head. The elf king and Wil walked to Danyl's home; the others remained at their stations and allowed the family to share in their grief. Entering the home, Hanna bowed to the king then followed Wil outside.

Alyxandyr pulled up a chair next to his grieving son. The room wavered for a moment and it was he who sat beside his dead queen's side. He held Anjya's hand, willing his love to open her eyes and rejoin those in the light. He had silently pleaded with her…begging her to return for their children's - and his - sake. His anguish was inconsolable. His children and his people gave him the strength and purpose to carry on. Danyl lost her once, but that only made this time all the more difficult. Alyxandyr collected his son in his arms and held him while he wept.

Zordana watched the chaos around her. The only chance she had of escaping was now. Blending in with the multitudes scrambling around in the city, she made her way to the eastern gate and disappeared.

Danyl sat on the bed beside Ramira. He held her limp hands while gazing at her pale face with bloodshot eyes. Her body remained warm hours after stabbing herself. That, he deduced, was probably due to the Source of Darkness inhabiting her body. He glanced at Kayla and Wyl sleeping peacefully next to their mother. The children continued to scream until the moment they snuggled up against Ramira. He blocked out all activities around him, including a distant whisper that resonated in the back of his mind. His anguish muted everything around him.

Sophie, Zada, Hanna, and Clare unobtrusively busied themselves by preparing a light meal while Allad, Seven, Alyxandyr, and Wil sat at the table.

The egg-shaped scar on Ramira's chest kept flashing in Zada's mind.

"What happened, Wil?" asked the king in a quiet voice.

Wil recounted everything that had occurred from the moment they woke up in the past, including meeting the first king. Silence reigned for several long minutes as the others grasped the monumental journey they had taken.

"What was he like?" asked Alyxandyr.

Wil leaned back in his chair. "His resolve to find a new home matched his dedication to the elves following him. His concern for our safety was always on his mind, too."

"How so?"

"He'd bring us food every day and extra blankets when needed, Seven," remembered Wil with a slight smile.

"Why are you smirking?"

"Because, Alyx, that elf tried everything to find out why we were there."

"The resemblance between him and Danyl was uncanny," added Hanna. "Wil actually called him Danyl when he nearly bumped into him."

"He immediately recognized Ramira. You should have seen her face when she realized what Suh's failed concoction accomplished." Wil stopped talking and took a sip of wine, the memory of Ramira's bloody body filling his vision.

"And when you returned to the present?" urged Alyxandyr.

Wil cleared his throat and then spoke in a soft yet clear voice. "Ramira detected the demons and rode over to confront them. She…she drove her blades into the mark on her chest and that's when she released the Black Queen's might."

The image pulsated in front of Zada's eyes again.

"Ramira told me to crush the amulet, which I did."

"The necklace was just a vessel for the black magic until it could infuse itself into Ramira," stated Allad.

"Magic cannot be extinguished…." began Clare.

"…but it can be altered," finished Zada.

The amulet's black stone continued to perplex her. There was something about it that seemed vaguely familiar. She had seen something like it before. The Herkah pursed her lips in thought. Blue lifted her head from the blanket; the white bandage stood out starkly against her black fur. Zada crouched beside the cat and stroked her head.

"You're a very brave girl, Blue."

Blue. The other stone was blue. Think, Zada, think! Blue stone…blue stone…blue stone. Ramira's bracelet was composed of blue beads into which the Lady of the Sands infused her memories to keep her safe from Mahn. Every bead that was broken revealed another moment in Ramira's life. Blue beads…blue beads made of glass.

Oblivious of those watching her, Zada's thoughts continued to churn. Sophie nudged Allad and then motioned to an unmoving Zada. Within moments all sound and movement ceased.

Cricket had a blue stone that reminded her of Ramira's bracelet! No one paid much attention to it after Cricket displayed it. What was its function?

Without warning, Zada's inner sight clicked on. She could 'see' Oma comforting a sobbing Ramira within the gloomy city of Thebes. Oma focused her gaze on the nomad, the unexpected hard look in her eyes filling Zada with dread. For a brief moment the brown woman's features shifted into something vague with sinister undertones. The vision abruptly ended.

"She's in danger," the nomad said.

"Who is?" asked Allad.

"Ramira."

"Ramira is dead," stated Allad.

Zada dashed up the stairs and yanked Danyl away from Ramira. She shook him out of his grief. "Danyl! Where's Cricket's stone?"

"What?" he stammered.

"The blue stone…where is it?"

"I…I don't know…why?"

Zada ran to the top of the stairs. "Everyone! Tear this place apart and find that blue stone! *Now!*"

Not knowing what they were looking for, they opened every drawer and cupboard in the house. The fruitless search continued. Sophie pushed aside the items on the mantle and found a small leather pouch. She opened the bag and peered inside.

"Here it is!"

Everyone crowded into the room and watched Zada hold the stone in her palm.

"What do we do with it? Break it like the beads on her bracelet?" asked a hopeful Danyl.

"That would be quite a memory," cautioned Allad.

"Whatever it's for, we have to figure that out very quickly," said Zada.

"Why?"

"Because, Danyl, Ramira's soul is in the clutches of something truly evil."

Ramira opened her eyes and looked up into a greenish sky veiled with thin, gray clouds. A pale, circular light shone down from the eerie sky. She lay upon something hard. Ramira sat up and looked around.

She stared with resignation at the granite walls towering over her and the fountains bordering the main avenue in Thebes. Nothing moved. Ramira headed toward the poor section and followed the narrow streets to Oma's home. If she were meant to spend an eternity in Thebes, at least she would find some measure of comfort there. Ramira stopped in front of the open door.

"Oma?" she called out while stepping into the house.

A fire crackled in the hearth where steam rose from the kettle hanging over the flames. The brown woman stepped out from behind the curtain and embraced Ramira. Her tears darkened Oma's shoulder.

"It's so good to have you home again, my sweet. Come." Oma led her to the table filled with food and drink, "Eat. You must be hungry after your long journey."

"I'm just tired, Oma."

The brown woman fixed her a plate of food and pushed it in front of Ramira. "Eat and then rest, my sweet."

Ramira stared at the honey and nut drizzled cakes. They were her favorite treats. She reached over and picked one up, never noticing the subtle fluctuation in Oma's face. Faint sounds echoed within the silent city.

"What's that?"

"Nothing, my sweet."

Curious, Ramira rose from the table and headed for the door.

"There's nothing out there," Oma called after her. "Come back inside, my sweet."

The glow from the peculiar sky bathed everything in a cold, greenish light. The scraping noises increased in volume. Ramira instinctively reached for her knives but found only empty sheaths. She spun around to question Oma and came face to face with her worst nightmare. The vaporous form of the Black Queen hovered a few scant feet away.

Ramira summoned forth the Source of Darkness but the magic would not comply. She looked around and watched in horror as the evil souls of the demons materialized out from the gloomy recesses of the buildings. Flight was her only choice. She dashed back up the avenue, out the main gate, and headed for the mountain range, separating the desert from the Broken Plain. Hundreds of demons forced her in the direction of a rocky slope that materialized through the greenish gloom.

Panicking, Ramira desperately searched for a place to hide but saw only a wide, flat plain. With nowhere else to run, she scrambled up the jagged face. The escarpment narrowed as she climbed; her hands and feet bled freely from the sharp edges. Loose stones and gravel gave way as she struggled up the sides. Her frightened ascension abruptly ended. Panting hard, she found herself on a pinnacle of rock beneath a greenish sky. Grayish clouds drifted overhead partially concealing a bright light. Ramira glanced down - only a scant few feet separated her from the Brethren.

The Brethren moved as one in a counter-clockwise direction and formed a silent eddy of malevolence. Blood continued to drip off the cuts on Ramira's exposed skin. The Black Queen drifted to within arms' reach. Ramira glared at the Black Queen in defiance.

"You have the blood of thousands upon your hands," stated the Black Queen. "You are one of us."

"No."

The Black Queen lifted a brow then waved her hand over the circling demons. A murky haze materialized, momentarily concealing them before reforming into a whirlpool filled with faces that Ramira recognized. Oma. Imhap. Horemb. Nyk. Karolauren. Elves, dwarves, Herkahs, and men rose from the gloomy miasma only to retreat within the churning vapor.

"Their deaths are *your* doing."

Ramira shook her head.

A cold and evil chuckling echoed across the shadowy plains. "You even killed your own children."

"*No!*"

"Take my hand and become who you were meant to be."

"I will never accept you," hissed Ramira.

The Black Queen cocked her head and laughed. "I *am* you."

"But I am not *you*."

"You're trapped…why delay the inevitable?"

The Black Queen was correct. Without her magic or black blades, and surrounded by the demons, Ramira was at the queen's mercy. Uncertainty rippled through her mind; her eyes radiated a haunted feeling.

"That's right. Take my hand."

The faces of the dead erupted up from the spectral current and cast silent accusations at her. Tears trickled down her cheeks.

"The guilt will be erased…all you have to do is accept me."

Ramira's hand slowly lifted; she gazed despondently at the pale-yellow disk partially obscured by the wispy clouds. It pulsed weakly.

"That's it…be who you were meant to be," encouraged the Black Queen as she reached out toward Ramira. "Let go of the fake identity you created to alleviate your culpability in their deaths."

For a brief moment, the ominous landscape was replaced with another scene…

She and Oma escaped the stifling confines of the house and retreated to the rooftop of Oma's home. Stars shone down from a moonless night sky. A warm yet refreshing breeze dried the perspiration on their skin.

I can't see you, Oma.

All I need is the light in my heart to see you with, my sweet…

Something flared to life in Ramira's breast. It coursed throughout her body and shattered the uncertainty and fear shackling her to the moment. Ramira had no idea what was going to happen to her spirit, but she was not going to submit to the evil threatening to crush her. This was her final stand. This moment defined her not as she was born but who she chose to be. She would accept her fate on her terms.

Yanking her hand away from the Black Queen, Ramira lifted her arms up and faced the watery light with a newfound resolve. She strained toward the watery disk even though the thickening clouds began to obscure it.

~

Kayla and Wyl whimpered in their sleep, drawing the attention of those in the room. Danyl cocked his head then grabbed the lantern on the night stand. Holding it close to Ramira's face, the light reflected off a fine sheen of perspiration.

"Dead people don't sweat," stated Wil.

"If she's not dead, then where is she?"

"Her soul is trapped, Danyl," replied Zada.

"But where?" demanded the elf prince.

"In the heart of darkness."

"You saw this?" asked Danyl.

"Yes."

The blue stone filled Wil's vision and silenced the frantic discussions around him. It reminded him of the faceted black jewel that hung from the Ankh-Nam. The size and shape were identical even though the surfaces were not. Was it ever part of a necklace? He glanced at Ramira then back to the stone. A subtle encouragement echoed in his mind.

"The scar," breathed Wil.

The loud disagreement drowned out the brigand's words.

Wil pushed past the elf and yanked the sheet off Ramira's chest. Lamplight reflected off the glistening droplets of blood on the raw wound.

"The scar!" he yelled dropping the stone into Danyl's hand.

They all stared at Wil.

"Danyl! Place the stone on the wound!"

The elf hesitated while looking to Zada for guidance. She opened her mouth but remained silent. Impatient, Wil snatched the stone from Danyl's hand and placed it on the wound. Nothing happened. He took a deep breath and then jammed the stone into the gash. Enraged, Danyl seized the back of Wil's tunic and began to pull him back when the stone began to glow. First one, then dozens of blue sparkles erupted from the gem and disappeared into her body.

Wil watched the glow spread outward through her veins. The memory of the blackness surging through Ramira's veins in Doth-Khan resurfaced. He prayed that he had not committed a grave error.

~

The Black Queen's reaction was immediate. She screeched in defiance and lunged at Ramira. The impact forced Ramira onto the ground where she and the Black Queen continued to brawl. The Black Queen struggled to absorb Ramira's soul; Ramira battled to retain it. There was no physical connection to the outside world this time. It was up to Ramira to break free if she wanted to live in the light. She violently shoved the Black Queen away. The Black Queen panted and glared at Ramira, who stood tall, ready to resume the fight for her soul.

"We could do this for eternity," shouted the Black Queen.

"I'll never yield to you."

"You have no choice."

"There's always a choice," declared Ramira.

Frustrated, the Black Queen pointed at the Brethren. "I'll let them rip you apart and then gorge on your tattered soul!"

The Brethrens' circular movement ceased. The Black Queen followed Ramira's gaze toward the dwindling light. The Black Queen's sneering laughter punctuated the silence.

*All I need is the light in my heart to see you with, my sweet…*echoed in Ramira's mind.

"Do you actually think that the mortals will help you?"

Ramira closed her eyes and opened her heart.

"I've had enough," shouted the Black Queen.

The faint light in Ramira's heart flared and then took on a bluish cast. Unafraid, she permitted it to extend throughout her body. It crackled and sizzled with a mysterious energy. Ramira opened her eyes, which glowed with an unearthly blue light. The power continued to build-up in her soul until it begged for release. Lifting her arms up,

Ramira discharged the blue might. The Source of Darkness flared to life and mingled with the other power. Thousands of threadlike beams ripped into the demons and Black Queen, incinerating them forever. Their brief shrieks continued to echo for several long moments before silence descended upon the plain.

Standing alone in the near darkness, Ramira looked up at the pinpoint of light. Her way out was too far away and she was too drained to try.

Ramira could only stare at the diminishing light. She looked around in the semi-darkness; silence threatened to tear away at her faltering courage. Tears rolled down her cheeks when she realized that she would spend eternity in this barren place. Sitting down on the ground, she brought her knees to her chest and wrapped her arms around them.

~

Having expended all of its energy, the jewel simply dispersed. Silence echoed within the bedroom as those gathered waited for any reaction from Ramira. The minutes ticked by, yet she remained unresponsive. A sense of panic began to erupt in those gathered around the bed. Kayla and Wyl continued to whimper.

"Why is she not responding?" asked Danyl in a choked voice. "Zada?"

The nomad shrugged and then slipped her hand into Ramira's. Try as she might, her inner sight refused to open.

"Can you 'see' her, Zada?"

"No, Danyl; my sight cannot penetrate into the eternal darkness."

"Why not?" he pressed.

"Only the dead can venture there," she explained. *Or a wraith.*

"What do we do now?" he asked in an anxious tone. "We can't leave her there."

A whitish haze began to form beside Wil. Fascinated, Zada discerned the ethereal form of a beautiful woman with long hair materializing beside him. The shade gazed lovingly at Wil for a moment and then floated to the babies. She reached out and brushed her fingers across Wyl's cheek then repeated the gesture on Kayla's face. The specter nodded to her, Wil, and Danyl.

"Everyone except for Danyl and Wil must leave," whispered Zada.

Danyl and Wil stared at Zada while she watched something they could not see. Astonishment fluctuated across her calm features. Their mystified looks morphed into shock when the ghost revealed herself to them.

"*Ma…*," breathed Wil, the urge to embrace her overwhelming him.

Zaura smiled at her son and then resumed a nebulous appearance. The silvery white haze seeped into Ramira's body.

"That's your mother?" asked Danyl.

His emotions stealing his voice, Wil could only nod.

Ramira gazed longingly at the point of light in the darkening sky. Too exhausted, she remained seated on the unyielding ground. A flicker of light caught her attention. She slowly stood as the silvery white glow approached her. Ramira watched the wavering shape transform into a lovely woman with long hair. She instinctively recognized her.

You do not belong here, Ramira.

"I don't have the strength to go back, Zaura."

I have enough for the both of us.

The shade held out her hand. Unafraid, Ramira took it. Like smoke rising from a fire, they drifted up toward the light. Ramira ignored the receding darkness and concentrated instead on the expanding disc. The farther they rose, the brighter the light became. Soon, a comforting whiteness blotted out the eternal gloom far below…

The hard ground was replaced with softness; the cold, musty air dissipated. Familiar voices filled her ears; she felt two tiny bodies pressed against her side. Her senses picked up other things. A warm hand clung to hers…the scent of leather and traces of soap…the faint tinkling of silver bracelets…peppermint tea. She was home. *Thank you, Zaura.*

Danyl, Wil, and Zada leaned forward and held their breath while waiting for Ramira to open her eyes. Blinking several times, Ramira focused on the anxious trio hovering over her. She reached for Kayla and Wyl slumbering by her side. Overwhelmed, tears streamed down her cheeks. Danyl held her while she purged her nightmares; Wil and Zada hugged briefly before the nomad left to give the others the good news.

Wil sat in a chair and rested his elbows on his thighs. Staring at his clasped hands, he thought of his mother. She was watching all along. Shame regarding his past reddened his cheeks; a gentle touch brought him back to the present. Wil looked into his mother's benevolent face. Unconditional love shone from her eyes. She placed her ethereal hand against his heart; he rested his over hers and sighed. Smiling, the presence sparkled and then vanished. Wil continued to gaze at the empty space for several long moments.

"How are you feeling?" asked Danyl, wiping away her tears.

"Grateful to be here," she whispered hoarsely. She looked around. "Where's Hanna? Was she hurt?"

"No, she's fine," replied Wil in subdued tones. "I'll go get her."

"The souls of the damned are no more, Danyl. I wielded a strange blue light and destroyed them all."

"Cricket's stone gave you that power."

"I don't understand."

"It was the antithesis of the black jewel on the Ankh-Nam," explained Danyl.

Ramira gingerly fingered the wound. "How did you know to place it here?"

"I didn't…it was Wil."

"I'm glad that I didn't kill him on Caldon Island or at any point thereafter," she admitted.

"Me, too."

"They almost won, Danyl."

"I know, my love."

"I expended every last bit of the Source of Darkness to destroy them. The knives, too, are no more."

He stroked her hair. "I have a feeling that you won't be needing them anymore."

Her gaze strayed to Hanna standing in the doorway. Danyl waved her to his seat. Hanna took Ramira's hand.

"I'm glad that you are unharmed, Hanna."

"As am I. How are you feeling?"

"I'll be up and about soon."

"I'd like to help out until then."

Ramira nodded tiredly.

"I'll be downstairs."

"I'll give you two a few minutes," stated Danyl then followed Hanna to the kitchen.

Wil took her hand and kissed it. She wiped away the single tear rolling down his cheek.

"Are you crying, Pirate?"

"No…there's too much dust floating around. The lady of the house should clean more often."

"You'll pay dearly for that insult."

He smiled at her.

"Your mother rescued me from the eternal darkness."

Wil swallowed hard while struggling to keep the tears at bay. "I was able to see her one last time."

Ramira brushed away the grief rolling down his face. "Thank you for saving my soul, Wil."

He cleared his throat. "Keeping up with you is exhausting. I don't know how Danyl manages it."

"You need someone that exhausts *you*."

"I have someone in mind."

"Someone that revealed a great deal of resolve?"

"Someone that's *almost* as exasperating as you are," he replied with a wink.

"Don't lose Hanna, Pirate."

"I don't intend to."

"That's the smartest thing I've ever heard you say," she said in a weary voice.

Wil kissed her forehead. "Get some rest."

Wil tucked the blanket around Kayla and Wyl. He hesitated then sat down on the bed again.

"Suh was convinced that my mother was a wraith, Ramira," he revealed in a quiet voice.

"It's true, Wil."

He stared at her. "How long have you known?"

"Since the morning after our son was born when you told me your mother's true name."

"Who told you?"

"Abby."

"What does Abby have to do with all of this?"

"She was your mother's sister, as was Zistak, the wraith Suh drained of her blood."

Wil's mouth opened but no sound came out.

"Abby betrayed both her sisters, which is why your mother ran away and hid from Abby. Your mother never told you the truth because she didn't want any harm to come to you, Wil. In a way, I guess that was my thought, too."

A flicker of hurt crossed his features. "I'm a grown man, Ramira. I could have handled the truth."

"I'm sorry, Wil."

He watched her struggle to remain awake; the huskiness in her voice became more pronounced. Her journey had continued to a terrible place he never wanted to go to. Wil's disappointment faded away and was replaced with reverence for the woman who gave everything to keep them all safe.

"You have nothing to be sorry for, Ramira," he whispered to her as she finally fell asleep.

ELEVEN

Widows Point bustled with activity as the riders headed down the main avenue. Tong fingered the forgotten vial of orange sparkles in his pocket and grinned. The uneventful trek back ended for Jules that morning. Sprinkling just a few grains of the powder into Jules's tea left her unable to speak and very compliant. Tong yanked on the rope tied to Jules' wrists and jerked her alongside his horse. People stopped and stared at her, some uttering vulgar comments while still others pointed and laughed. Jules' greasy hair and road grime clung to her skin; the stench from her long unwashed body hovered around her in an invisible cloud. All she could muster was a mask of arrogance.

Tong tugged the rope and rode down a winding side street toward the seedier side of town. The relative orderliness of the main street morphed into ramshackle buildings in need of repair. He halted several turns later in front of a three-story building with open porches on the second and third floors. Men and women in various stages of undress leered down at them. The pirate turned to Jules, whose face drained of all color. Tong offered the stout woman with too much make-up and yellowed teeth a brief nod then handed over the end of the rope. He passed the vial to her as well.

"Just a few grains added to a liquid once a day will keep her *accommodating*, Madam."

"Obliged, Tong."

Kicking the sides of his horse, Tong rode down the main avenue and to the *Gray Wolf*. He would be on the Spice Islands within three days. Tong smiled.

~

Danyl opened the door for Wil and Hanna. He invited them in then took their cloaks and hung them by the fireplace. Hanna wore a burgundy gown edged with gold thread; she wore her hair in a thick braid down her back. A pair of rubies dangled from her gold filigree earrings. Wil wore a dark gray pair of trousers and a lighter gray woolen top.

"You look beautiful, Hanna!"

"Thank you, Danyl."

Kayla waddled over and reached for Wil. He picked her up and hugged her then kissed his son who napped under Blue's watchful gaze. The cat purred loudly when he scratched her chin.

"Would you mind keeping an eye on the children for a moment, Hanna? Wil and I need to talk to Ramira."

"Not at all."

Danyl and Wil headed upstairs to the bedroom and watched Ramira brush her hair. She gathered it in a braid and secured it with Jack's silver hair clip. She placed her hands on her hips and looked with suspicion from one to the other.

"What are you two fools up to?"

"We have something for you."

"Why?"

"Does there have to be a reason?" asked Wil.

She approached them and waited. Wil fished a small leather pouch from his pocket and handed it to her. Both elf and man watched her untie the cords and deposit the item into her palm.

Ramira picked up one end of the silver chain and held the locket up to eye level. Larger than a cherry, the highly polished pale green stone was flat on one side and rounded on the other. Tiny veins of black and white quartz provided a beautiful contrast. Ramira's gaze traveled to the men and back again.

"Open it," urged Danyl.

Ramira undid the silver clasp and looked at the locket's contents. Five distinct locks of hair formed a single braid; several grains of white sand were contained behind a glass casement. Ramira's hands trembled when she brushed her fingertip against the braid. Danyl took the necklace and fastened it around her neck.

"Seven quarried the stone from the heart of Evan's Peak and Zada brought the grains from the heart of the Great White Desert. The chain belonged to my mother," explained Danyl. "Wil spent hours polishing it."

"It was less arduous than trying to start a fire…or that other thing."

Ramira grinned as the memories flooded back. The locket filled her vision until her tears blurred it.

"Do you like it?" they quietly asked in unison.

She hugged and kissed Danyl and then Wil. "It's perfect."

The three went downstairs and joined Hanna and the children for their journey to the castle. Danyl and Ramira carried their children while Wil escorted Hanna to the dining hall in the castle. Hanna gripped his arm tightly as she glanced around the hallway decorated with candles of varying heights. Twigs bearing colorful leaves and pine cones surrounded the lights; the delicious aroma of baked apples filled the hallway. Blue limped alongside Wil. They followed the attendant to a set of double doors that opened the moment they reached them. They entered the reception area and were warmly greeted by the dwarf and Herkah couples, Sophie, Mason, Styph, Alyssa, and Alyxandyr. The Elven king hugged his grandchildren and beamed with joy. Laughter and conversation echoed within the room as old and new friends met. Individuals freely mingled with one another regardless of station.

Alyxandyr excused himself and motioned Wil to the far corner of the room.

"Wil, my boy," began the king in a quiet voice, "we need to discuss a situation."

Confusion rippled across the brigand's face, for even he knew that business was never mentioned at these celebrations. Alyxandyr placing his arm across Wil's shoulders mystified him even more.

"How long have you been a thorn in my side?"

"Umm…for far too long?"

"Not quite as long as my children have been, but you've managed to make up for lost time."

"I don't know how to answer that, Alyx."

"You are not in any trouble."

Wil felt a sense of relief.

"Not yet, anyway. I make it a point to stay current on the goings-on in the city and you know what? That's easier than what happens in my own household."

Wil's mouth went dry.

"Do you know why, Wil?"

Wil shook his head.

"Because my children are quite adept at keeping secrets from me."

Wil's thoughts turned to the knowledge that he, Danyl, and Ramira shared.

"Not all of them, mind you. Well, Styph and Danyl are the usual culprits. Do you think me a fool, Wil?"

"Absolutely not!"

The Elven king stared into Wil's unblinking eyes. Wil's subtle panic was not lost on the king, who slowly smiled at the brigand.

"What is this all about, Alyx?"

"Your future."

The king's face conveyed a friendly conversation with Wil, whose back was turned toward the others.

"What's Father discussing with Wil, Danyl?" Styph asked.

"I don't have a clue, but you know the conversations we've had with Father when *he* has his arm around *our* shoulders."

"All too well," replied the crown prince.

"Should we save him?"

Styph casually glanced over at the two deep in conversation. "Would he do it for one of us?"

"Yes."

The brothers flanked Wil and listened to the king's proposal.

"What do you two think about making Wil an honorary prince? He has, after all, greatly contributed to the protection of all the Races."

"So he'll share in our duties?" asked Styph.

"Some of them, yes."

"Does that mean I can one day become king?" queried Wil.

"No," replied Alyxandyr. "It means you will, however, be officially a member of the royal household."

"I would be honored."

Sitting on a loveseat away from the others, Ramira held her sleeping son while her daughter lay curled up in her lap. She kissed Wyl's forehead and stroked Kayla's auburn hair. Ramira's gaze shifted amongst those gathered. Seven, Allad, and Styph shared a laugh; Wil, Danyl, Hanna, and Clare clustered around Zada. Ramira could hear the silvery tinkling of the nomad's bracelets whenever she lifted her hands. Alyssa whispered something into her father's ears; Sophie and Mason shared a few words. A contented sensation overwhelmed her, especially when Danyl excused himself and sat down beside her. He gathered his son in his arms and soothingly ran his hand up and down Wyl's back. Blue hobbled over and sat down in front of them. Her green eyes focused on whoever spoke.

"What are you thinking about?"

For a brief moment she stood upon the pinnacle of rock beneath a gloomy sky. Oma's soothing voice echoed in her mind. *All I need is the light in my heart to see you with, my sweet.* The far-away look in Ramira's eyes matched the tone of her voice.

"Facing my dark side was a painful and sobering undertaking, Danyl, especially without my blades and magic. Frightened and beleaguered, I nearly gave in to it."

"What stopped you?"

"A memory of Oma reminding me that the mightiest weapon isn't composed of metal or magic but of faith."

Danyl spoke in the old elvish tongue, the words comforting even though she did not understand them.

"What does that mean?"

"A pure soul will survive the endless hours of darkness."

Ramira leaned toward Danyl and kissed him.

"Father is going to make Wil an honorary prince."

"From orphan to pirate to royalty…please tell me that he won't be in line for the throne!"

Danyl chuckled and shook his head.

"Now all we have to do is get him to wed Hanna."

They turned their attention to Wil, who whispered into Hanna's ear. Smiling in response, she brushed her fingertips against his cheek.

"I'm guessing that will happen in the near future," said Danyl.

Alyssa motioned them into the dining hall where the staff placed domed platters on the serving table against the wall. Danyl and Ramira lay their sleeping children in the crib near the fireplace and then stood in front of their chairs. Wil and Hanna occupied the seats to her right. Candles, bowls of fruit and nuts, and squat vases holding flowers provided a festive centerpiece. The candlelight reflected off the glassware. Plain white dinnerware rested on a pale green tablecloth. The Elven king lifted his wine glass.

"I consider everyone at this table my family and I am proud to announce that Wil has been chosen to become an honorary prince."

Looks of approval and congratulations circulated around the table. Wil lifted his glass to the king and to everyone else. He took a deep breath to control his emotions then turned his attention back to Alyxandyr.

"I am surrounded by old friends and new ones," the king continued. "Our survival compelled us to seek each other out, and our shared beliefs gave us the courage to stem the darkness that threatened to extinguish our existence. Our Elven ancestors barely escaped that same threat a thousand years ago." Alyxandyr's gaze fixed on Ramira for a brief moment.

A subtle smile lifted the corners of Hanna's mouth. The memory of meeting the first king and his reaction to Ramira made this king's words that much more powerful. One woman's decision changed the course of history. She glanced at Ramira, who politely excused herself to attend to her whimpering son. Wyl ceased crying the moment his mother picked him up. Hanna marveled at Ramira's steadfast convictions to her family and friends. These tenets appeared contradictory to the magic and blades Ramira wielded without mercy or regret. A newfound respect for Ramira filled Hanna's heart. Wil's finger brushing against her hand brought her back to the present.

"Those same principles allowed us to endure one last stand against the darkness," resumed Alyxandyr.

Zada's attention turned to Ramira, who discreetly resumed her place between Danyl and Wil. Both men were instrumental in saving her soul and, through her, the land. Wil and Hanna experienced something that no mortal ever had or, she surmised, ever would again. Her gaze shifted to all those gathered at the table. Elf, dwarf, Herkah, and man each gave all they could to keep everyone safe. The fabric of life was composed of many woven threads.

"None of us, however, would be standing here had it not been for Ramira's selfless acts."

Hidden behind one of the pleats on her gown, Ramira's hand sought Danyl's. He slipped his fingers around hers and gave them a reassuring squeeze.

"We are all in your debt once more."

An uncomfortable sensation rippled through Ramira when her family and friends lifted their glasses to her. The feeling worsened when the king asked her to speak a few words. She looked at her children, willing one of them to cry and save her from the moment. They continued, however, to slumber peacefully in the crib.

Ramira glanced around the table and met everyone's steady gaze with an open heart. Sophie's kindness and Seven's cheerfulness blended perfectly with Zada's wisdom and Alyxandyr's steadfastness. Allad's and Clare's uncompromising devotion to their loved ones and Hanna's friendship were palpable. Ramira and Wil exchanged a discreet look; she turned to Danyl, the love of her life. There were no words she could utter to convey the profound feelings bubbling within her. *All I need is the light in my heart to see you with, my sweet.*

Friends and family watched in astonishment as Ramira backed away from the table and bowed deeply to them. The necklace slipped out from her bodice and swung back and forth.

The necklace caught Seven's attention. The truth behind Danyl's secretive request was finally revealed. The prince's love for Ramira would forever be linked to Evan's Peak and, Seven suspected, with all of Danyl's friends and family. It was fitting that Ramira – who saved them all from annihilation – wore such a simple yet powerful symbol of their unity. The dwarf king bowed his head to Ramira.

EPILOGUE

Holding torches to light the way, Ramira, Hanna, and Wil followed the guard down the dark stairway toward the royal crypt. Their shadows wavered against the stone wall; the air became heavier. Sounds diminished until only their footsteps and breathing echoed off the walls. They stopped in front of a pair of wide doors and nodded to the honor guard flanking the entrance. The elves opened the doors. The sentry led them past rows of sarcophagi, which contained the bodies of past kings and queens until they reached the far corner of the vast chamber. Placing the brands in brackets, the elf bowed his head and gave them their privacy.

Alyxandyr's and Annal's likenesses were carved into the stone. The first king ordered that she would be interred with him. He held a sword across his heart with one hand and clasped Annal's hand with the other.

Wil thought back to when he almost bumped into Alyxandyr. The elf's uncompromising stare bore right through him. Thinking back, Wil realized it was that indomitable spirit that allowed the elves to survive and endure. The man was grateful that the elf succeeded. And that he had the chance to actually meet him.

"Alyxandyr died of pneumonia thirty years after establishing Bystyn," whispered Hanna. "Annal ruled for another ten years before she, too, succumbed to the same sickness. Their daughter, Aryal, became queen. It was she who doggedly pursued her father's dream."

Ramira gazed upon Alyxandyr's image. The memory of the conversation regarding him trying to impress his brothers surfaced in her mind. His tenacity was on display even as a young boy. It would serve him well later on in his life. Their words echoed in her mind.

Do you believe in fate?

Don't you, Alyxandyr?

I do now.

The sputtering torches brought her back to the present. She looked at Wil and Hanna and then nodded. It was time to go. As one, the trio backed away from the sarcophagus and bowed deeply to the first Elven king. The guard escorted them from the crypt and back up to the land of the living.

www.ingramcontent.com/pod-product-compliance
Lightning Source LLC
Chambersburg PA
CBHW070828180626
46818CB00001B/440